Behind Each Face

Dear Cruz,

To a woman who advocates for many people used esteem.

Honored to be family.

Julie

Behind
Each
Face

... bearing witness ...

JULIA PENNER-ZOOK

Behind
Each
Face

Copyright © 2015 by Julia Penner-Zook

Sapphire Dance Press

ISBN: 978-0-9964873-0-6

Printed by CreateSpace, An Amazon.com Company

Some of the stories contained in **Behind Each Face** are strictly fiction. Where actual stories are conveyed, the names of all individuals have been changed and identifying features, including physical descriptions, occupations and locations have been modified in order to preserve their anonymity. In some cases, composite characters have been created in order to further preserve the privacy and to maintain narrative flow. The goal in all cases was to protect people's privacy without damaging the integrity of the story.

Contents

Acknowledgements   i
Foreword   v
Preface   ix
The Stories

Vortex on 152nd 1
The Black Beetle   5
Mirror, Mirror on the Wall   11
Body Slam   15
Golden Grief   21
Gutted   27
Just Another Court Hearing   33
Hearing Voices   37
Taffeta Sailor   43
Season's Pleadings   47
9 a.m. Monday   53
Darkness   57
Easter's Lavender   61
Paints, Palettes and Pathos   67
Ninety-Nine   71
Hoods   77
Removing Labels   81
She Spoke My Name   87
That Small Child   91
Sapphire Trae McKesson   97
Under Cover of Darkness   103
Daddy, I Got This   107
Whose Truth?   111
By Your Words   115
Transcendence   121

Contents Continued

After the Final Curtain   127
About the Author   129

Acknowledgements

I am deeply grateful to the following people:

➤ Jill Ockhardt, professional editor, who was not afraid to apply her *editorial red pen* liberally to tighten syntax and to challenge my literary judgment as it pertained to character development and flow. She is a tremendous resource;

➤ Stacey L. Rhoades, accomplished *photographer*, who took hundreds of photographs, then edited them for front and back covers. She has been a tireless advisor on visual components;

➤ each person willing to have their *photo* taken for the cover, helping to create the visual diversity reflected in this compilation of stories;

➤ Rod Zook who spent hours deciphering my cryptic vision for the *cover* and then bringing creative order to dozens of photographs;

➤ the twelve women who graciously contributed to the *Foreword*. Your participation represented enormous goodwill and support for this work;

➤ numerous friends and family members, who repeatedly read story after story, asking clarifying questions and making suggestions;

➤ many social services professionals and

colleagues from whom I've learned so much over many years;

➤ various bloggers, artists, poets and writers who have expressed encouragement, excitement and support;

➤ those who have written personal emails, notes on social media and asked about progress by phone;

➤ everyone who at any point in the past few years has asked, "Have you ever thought of writing a book?" A special thank you for the question, "What qualifies you to write?" I am a better writer as a result.

➤ a short list of writers who, among many, have inspired and shaped me: Dr. Maya Angelou, Joshua Safran, Cynthia Bond, Alice Munro, Fr. Richard Rohr, Barbara Brown Taylor and Christine Baker Kline.

➤ people who've given above and beyond:

- my husband, Rod, who has been an advisor and advocate, given me space to write, been patient through the tedium, preoccupation, frustration and exuberance of the process, and who has been encouraging along every step of this journey;

- my sisters, Marilyn and Jenny, who have given emotional support and objective feedback;

- Stacey, who is a friend, listener, professional

advisor, visionary and someone who always says, "You can do this!";

. Melissa, a fellow writer, who has repeatedly asked, "How is your project coming?";

. women who've given me permission to use (and alter) their very personal stories;

Thank you! Truly, I would not have been able to complete this—and feel good about it—without each of you!

Foreword

As I reflected on what the Foreword could encompass, I decided to invite a number of women to speak out of their life experiences. Twelve wonderfully capable and insightful women agreed to participate. I'm so grateful to each of them, and to those who deliberated, and for whatever reason, were unable to contribute.

The broad strokes for their consideration were either to describe an experience that shaped their concern for the health, safety and wellbeing of women and girls, or to reflect on an ingredient that contributed to their own strength (or a missing element that could have strengthened them).

The responses were heartwarming. Please enjoy this personal introduction to ***Behind Each Face.***

＞

＞ I'd like to repeat high school. Not because I didn't get the lead in the musical or asked to prom. It's because no one told me I was a beautiful, capable woman. I wish more young women could realize they are gifted, and worthy of love and being taken seriously.

Nancy Eberly

＞ Key ingredients that have made me a stronger woman are compassion and love. When I exercise these qualities, whether toward others or myself, I feel grounded and free. Because we are imperfect, compassion and love are required to let go of pain, anger and resentment. This builds hope and faith.

Annie Tshimika-Edmunds

➤ Through the influence of others—parents, family members and friends—I've had examples of what it means to be strong, spiritually committed, faithful, enthusiastic and creative. As a result I've been able to become a strong, persevering, trusting woman—one who lives life to the full daily.

Marilyn Braun

➤ An important component of strength is the ability to have absolute trust, even in the most adverse situations. If trust is resolute, a strong woman knows she will be able to navigate every change, transition, as well as all confusing situations, confident that each experience contributes to the greatest good.

Marla Joy Hoffman

➤ I have spent the majority of my life crippled by fear of being truly seen—flaws and all. When I reconciled with my own brokenness and facades, I came to peace with *perfect imperfection*. Therein lies strength. Through God's empowering, I share my story so others can also experience freedom.

Kim Molinari

➤ My mother lost her mother when she was five years old, but she became a strong woman of faith. She then blessed me with her encouragement to venture out and try new things. She always supported me in my endeavors and was an awesome role model for me.

Susan Rhoades

⤙ Thirty years ago I watched Jean Kilbourne's groundbreaking film "Killing Me Softly" which points out advertising's depiction of women as sex objects. I realized more profoundly than ever that women I knew—myself included—were so much more. We were intelligent, passionate, caring people. This revolutionized my view of advertising.

Nadine Miller

⤙ My pivotal moment came at puberty, when my father died suddenly. I felt the weight of responsibility descend on me—alone in a vast world of only me, and my young mother. It was I who silently supported that brave woman, helping her long life become a song of strength.

Joanne Kohut

⤙ There is a unique sort of resiliency in all women: physically, spiritually, emotionally, and intellectually. As women, we are blessed with many opportunities to experience change, challenge, and triumph. It is our resiliency as women that gives us our strength to conquer all that life has to offer.

Melissa Sharp

⤙ Discovered behind closed doors, covered in her own blood, this young teen girl had become unable to endure further suffering, abuse and absence of love.

In the ambulance, caring for her physical wounds, I determined to impact young people's lives: to hear their pain, guide and counsel them to wholeness.

Stacey Rhoades

➤ My mother's sudden death broke me. Many parts of me, that I thought only she could fill, withered. Over time, I filled those parts. It was her voice that guided me, but it was my strength, resiliency, and love for myself and my sister that put the pieces back together.

Jeanine Overton

➤ Her arrival jolted our naïve dreams of grandparenthood: Down syndrome. Wise counsel, while embracing this complexity, suggested she could realize greater potential than we might anticipate. So it has been. Her sheer joy of life, guileless lack of pretense and profound empathy continually point to what I, too, might become.

Jenny Regehr

Preface

Welcome to *Behind Each Face*.

Thank you for choosing to read the Preface before venturing into the heart of the book. Or possibly you've chosen to visit here after already dipping your toes into the stories. Either way, I'm delighted you came.

With this *Preface*, I hope to pull back the curtain–giving you a glimpse into the broader motivation behind the words contained in the stories. Here's a backdrop to make the most of your reading experience.

Behind Each Face*
—is a compilation of stories dedicated to girls and women, and to those who wish to see them overcome, flourish and thrive.

This project was born out of years of stories witnessed.

Stories heard
on planes
in classrooms
in church basements
one-on-one in quiet places
after public events
over coffee
in parks

in courtrooms
on the phone.

Every one—mundane, magical or miserable—
is valuable. Without equal and priceless.
So many women's and girls' stories
would never see the light of day ...
often strictly confined
to the ear of a confidant,
a fellow traveler,
a healthcare or social services professional,
... were it not for someone—
anyone with an open soul
and an active pen—
to give them life.
To bear witness.

Here's to the women and girls of the stories
told in **Behind Each Face.**

⤙⤚

*The stories included in this compilation appear in the
form of*
Flash Fiction—*also known as* **Smoke Stories,**
*named this way simply because it's possible to read
one story in the time it
takes to smoke a cigarette.*

While there are numerous variations to the
general category of Flash Fiction, the one I've chosen
is a narrative of 1,000 words or fewer, telling a story
that can stand alone.
When I hear *1,000 words*, I immediately think

of the well-worn phrase in praise of the visual: a picture is worth a thousand words!

For a writer, the instant and effusive attention given to *a picture*—any picture—can be very intimidating. The question easily becomes: How can I "write more loudly" so that words will be noticed above the visual stimulation a picture offers?

The challenge that I as a writer of Flash Fiction have adopted is this:

no picture could ever present the vibrancy of expression that 1,000 words provide.

How will I know when I've reached the ***vibrancy of expression*** *that must accompany an effective Flash Fiction story?*

As with most artists, who choose to *live in public*—i.e. publish their work, place their work in exhibition, record or perform a piece of music—we will never think our work is done. The certainty that there is more to be polished or improved, tweaked or modified adheres to us like a permanent leech.

Recently I discovered a helpful gauge whereby an artist can determine the status of his/her work (I would love to give credit, but have been unable to find the source):

If you can still change something on your manuscript (piece of art) to clearly improve its

quality, you're not ready to publish, perform or
exhibit. When you have taken your work as far as
you can:
SHARE IT!

With the help of a capable community of
professional and personal contributors, I'm at that
point. I will share—not because this work is perfect,
but because I've taken this work as far as I can take
it! I'm honored to present to you...

Behind Each Face

Julia Penner-Zook
Summer 2015

* Note: the stories contained in this book are not the stories of
the people pictured on the book cover.

Bearing witness is a humbling, sobering, yet life-giving experience, both for the one who hears and for the one who speaks. Without a space in which a voice—a story—is honored, we live without meaning, growth, healing and understanding.

Behind Each Face
The Stories

Vortex on 152nd

>➤➤

Sounds of chirping birds, leaves gently rustling in giant oaks and the laughter of a waterfall surrounded her with velvety tranquility as she sat motionless on slightly overgrown concrete stairs just outside the park's furthest sanctuary building. She noticed none of it. For what seemed like hours, she sat there, unseeing eyes fixed on the scene before her.

What had just happened to her life in the past nine months? She had once been an adventure-seeking, vivacious nurse practitioner, bringing life wherever she went. Her outgoing warmth had gained her many friends in her neighborhood, at work and in her place of worship. Every spare moment was spent lavishing love on severely abused pit bulls at a nearby rescue. Life was full, and life was good.

The rugged outdoorsman she was introduced to at an over-forty's singles' event at church quickly became more than a friend. He was charming, polite, thoughtful and spoiled her at every turn. Her heart smiled. This was the part of her life that had been missing. She loved his sparkle and attentiveness. She, who had always been known for her level-headed rationalism, was soon deeply attached and undeniably in love. They married eight weeks later, not far from where she now sat. Under the same trees. Together with a small, intimate group of friends. The day filled with gratitude, joy and hope.

He moved into her tastefully renovated,

downtown condo, nestled in an eighty-year-old former train station, next to quaint cafes, artists' studios and bike repair shops.

In less than two weeks, however, she could hardly recognize what had been her soothing, delightfully eccentric home. He had taken over her office, where he spent hours playing video games. Her kitchen sink seemed permanently piled with used dishes, her bathroom floor littered with wet towels and dirty clothes. Soon, the hours away from her demanding profession were spent either with the needy pit bulls or in a living space where she was made to keep her music low, to fetch bottle after bottle of chilled Tooheys New, and to go to bed alone while he spent evenings in his recliner, finishing up "just this last game". In *her* office. Surrounded by empty bottles and pizza boxes.

She remembered their times of laughter, walks in the park, tall cool drinks in the bar, intimate conversations. Where was that now? When she reminisced out loud, he spat angrily that she was "laying on the guilt". In fact, he blamed her viciously for failing to keep the condo clean, for not having dinner ready at a "normal" hour (blustering that this was the reason he needed to resort to cheap, home-delivered pizza), and for not folding his clothes neatly in *his* drawers (which were in *her* dresser). He had no steady job, only part-time contracts when he decided to take them. But any attempt to come up with a plan to share various responsibilities ended with him accusing her of being entirely unreasonable, and with her desperately clinging to her integrity while articulating her perspectives.

She got up morning after morning, had her coffee, wrote romantic good-morning notes, tiptoed about the condo while hurrying to orient herself in each new day. Bills, errands and responsibilities—all falling behind. She scolded herself. She had always been on top of everything. Never late. Always together. But now, she seemed to lack the organization and focus to keep everything functioning.

He began to initiate scathing conversations about her lack of competence, her failure as a wife and her inability to manage finances. Her words were interrupted and twisted; her thoughts became disjointed; her heart, battered. Initially she had been horrified. Then hurt. Then frustrated. Finally, furious. This was *not* how she had envisioned a marriage with the love of her life.

Work suffered. Often it was weeks between visits to her beloved pit bulls. Ice filled her home and her life. One day she couldn't find a pair of earrings, given to her by her great-grandmother as she lay dying. Her query, "Honey, have you seen my amber earrings?" was met with, "How should I know where they are? I don't mess with your stuff!"

But, this was not an isolated incident. Disappearances became more frequent—everything from jewelry to her black evening gown, to the waffle iron. Even a pair of her designer dress shoes came up missing. Whenever she asked, responses were the same: "Look at this place. You couldn't keep track of anything in here. I didn't make you scatter-brained!"

His words seared her soul. His barrage of

accusations gnawed at her resiliency and confidence. His emotional distance pierced her heart. Her mental stability, vibrancy and competence were gone—all in just a few, short months. She sat alone, reeling. Staggering beneath the unbidden, undeserved burden.

Colleagues and friends noticed. They expressed concern. But it wouldn't be for several additional disorienting months, finding herself sitting there under the giant oaks, next to the waterfall, that she would wearily summon her strength to seek help. *This is not worth it*, she decided. *I've been alone before and I can do "alone" again.*

~~

Together the three of them climbed the stairs to the third floor condo and she opened the door. As if he had sensed impending doom, he had cleaned the entire condo—and himself—that day. No trace of beer bottles, unwashed dishes or pizza boxes. He was showered, shaved and impeccably dressed. She was momentarily stunned. Almost deterred. Had it not been for the two pillars next to her, she may have faltered. But their presence spurred her on. Sheer willpower forced the words from her lips: "Get out. Get out *now*."

What would follow was to become the most intense battle of her life to that point. But for now, there she stood. Weary and inwardly warped, but not destroyed. Definitely not destroyed.

The Black Beetle

It was always an embarrassment. It was old. Half the time it didn't work. It had once been black, now the rust had not only made it uglier, but had made driving hazardous. In the winter it simply became an extension of her family's deep freeze, as it didn't run anyway. It was her mother's disintegrating Volkswagen Beetle.

Vivienne—*not* Viv—knew her mother could not afford anything more, given the family's poverty. She single-handedly fed her and her four brothers: two older, two younger.

Poor. How she despised that word! Never enough. Making do. Constantly needing to "look normal" to maintain the carefree, satisfied and secure façade. But carefree, satisfied and secure were not her world.

Despite it all, Vivienne felt happy enough, though she stumbled home a mile and a quarter from school in all kinds of weather. The school bus didn't go to the very edge of town. It never neared her barren neighborhood, or "Scrapheap Hill" as she called it. Of course she never uttered those words out loud, fearing to draw attention to her unfortunate status.

Her mother worked two jobs to cover even the most basic living expenses for her family of six. When she was home, there were games, cookies, scrutinized homework assignments, steaming pots of soup, swift reprimands when they were out of line. And there was laughter—beautifully woven into the fabric of their frugal existence.

Vivienne was pulled in to help with household management from early on. She dusted, mopped, watered plants, chopped vegetables, did the laundry. In the summer she was the one to weed the garden—a dreaded task. What her brothers did was beyond her. The older two spent more time wandering the streets with friends than she ever could. The little ones depended on her to be cook, disciplinarian, nurse, tutor and whatever else *mothers* were supposed to do.

One scorching July afternoon after a particularly frustrating garden weeding episode, Vivienne determined she would not live like this. Not once she left home. Never. She would rise from this lowly, beetle-like condition and move up. Out. Forward. At twelve, these thoughts weren't elaborately formulated, but a steely determination was born. And it never left.

"Mom, Mrs. Wells has asked me to babysit the kids on Saturday night," she announced in the spring of the following year. Her mother's head snapped to face her.

"What? Babysit those three brats?"

"...and I said, 'yes'."

"How are you going to get there?"

"Mrs. Wells will pick me up and bring me home."

"You can't be home late. You have to sing in the choir on Sunday." Her mother had seen to it that her only daughter would take voice lessons *and* go to church. Vivienne complied with both demands. At least then.

"I told her that. I'll be home before midnight."

"Okay, but don't call me when those kids tear the house apart. I've seen them in the grocery store. Little devils."

Vivienne didn't pursue the conversation, already anxious about handling three lively youngsters. But she must go through with it. It would provide a little extra money. Maybe she could find more babysitting jobs to help move her forward.

She planned to eventually teach voice lessons, when her skill was at a level at which people could respect her as a teacher. She imagined that teaching music in her small town would prove difficult, as parents seldom encouraged their children to pursue music formally. Participation in every type of sport seemed a choice requiring less parental persuasion.

Week after week, Vivienne's ads ran: "Voice students wanted; reasonable price; at my house or yours." And remarkably she managed to fill every available time slot with students. In the winter she trudged through snow to teach those students who could not—or refused to—come to her. Later at night, when her mother was home, she babysat.

She taught, practiced, studied and babysat her way through middle school, then high school. Few suspected that her fertile mind was refining an intricate plan to propel herself toward independence. As her friends partied, flirted and chattered one year after another, she participated just enough to keep from appearing too different. But her plans came first. They were her lifeline. She needed those plans, unlike

7

some of her friends—the rich and privileged kids. She sighed when she thought of her friends. They couldn't be blamed, she lamented, but they were entirely naive and entitled. Later, as an adult, she would be more diplomatic. But not then. Not when every breath seemed to require exertion.

Vivienne pressed on. Hesitation was not an option. Neither was defeat. At nineteen she purchased her first car—cash. It wasn't pretty, and it had almost 100,000 miles on it, but it was *not* a Volkswagen Beetle. This vehicle made moving to a college dorm in the city possible. It was her connection with home on the weekends. It was her first sign that she could— yes, she *would* succeed.

She attended college on state scholarships and worked hard. Very hard. She managed to eke out A's throughout her bachelor of science program. Long before needing to apply for dental school, she began preparing for the Dental Admission Test, which she was frequently reminded was the downfall of many aspiring dental students. The exam was grueling. Vivienne would never forget the email she received announcing her passing grade while working late one evening at an exclusive wine bar in another part of the city. She shouted! Caused a scene! Danced in the kitchen! And her co-workers and patrons all toasted to her success. Tips were generous that night.

She would make it. Yes, she would. And she did.

Vivienne is now one of the leading dental surgeons in her state. Her mother retired comfortably years ago. Her brothers are in various parts of the country and are in touch occasionally. And Vivienne drives a sleek, new, black Volkswagen Phaeton.

Mirror, Mirror on the Wall

The day she was born was damp, cold and gray. The room musty, dark and cluttered. Commotion surrounded her birth—women bustling with water, towels, pillows and blankets. The one giving birth—anxious, sweaty, tired and blood stained. Just as the tiny, slippery bundle took her first howling breath, the door opened furiously, admitting the massive black-coated figure with a stiff, felt hat that concealed terrifyingly penetrating green eyes. No one knew why the local midwife chose this attire for her professional duties. And at this particular child's arrival, she was late.

Ms. Cole, dubbed "Black-As-Coal" by the townsfolk, cast aside her outerwear and lunged toward the new mother and her seconds-old baby girl. With the same wordlessness as she'd entered, she turned and plunged her hand into the soiled, frayed delivery bag that seemed an eccentric extension of her persona. Out came a tiny, rusted mirror, which she mysteriously held mere inches from the newborn's face. As the burly woman peered intently into the tiny face, the mother and attendants looked on in silent wonder. Why did she do that? Word on the street was that this was a common procedure at every birth Ms. Cole attended, but it seemed no one had ever dared question her about it directly. So this baffling ritual prevailed.

Baby Alexandra eventually became fascinated

with mirrors. Big mirrors, ornamental mirrors, mirrors in cars, plain mirrors, scratched or polished mirrors, mirrors on bicycles, in tiny backpacks, on neck chains. Her mother, a crude and scornful woman, attributed this inexplicable obsession to that first object, presented for her observation immediately after birth.

"Stop just standing there in front of that mirror!"

"Why are you looking at yourself again?"

"Don't you have anything better to look at?"

"You ain't beautiful, you know. Put that thing down!"

These and so many other disparaging remarks became wearisome—a doleful refrain that repeated in Alexandra's brain over and over and over. Like a scratched, worn-out vinyl recording.

Finally, Alexandra did "put that thing down," convinced there really was nothing about herself that was worthy of attention. Nothing outward, and therefore nothing on the inside. She wasn't beautiful—she'd heard that often enough. Nor was she particularly bright. She wasn't athletic or gifted in speech or song. She was plain. Unremarkable. Quite dull, really.

She began to trudge rather than walk. She dropped her gaze, looking at her feet rather than at her surroundings. She dressed in unassuming styles with subdued tones. Her existence became survival rather than joyful delight.

The thing was, those around her never noticed the change, because Alexandra was intuitively able to keep an even-keeled demeanor and an astonishingly gracious attitude when needed. No one suspected her inner turmoil and eroded confidence. The only tell-tale sign—had anyone been extraordinarily attentive—would have been that Alexandra never made a decision in a group and seemed to have an opinion about nothing. Because she had learned to dissolve into any circumstance, no one took note.

"So, what do you think of Alexandra?" Had that question ever been posed, the one questioned would certainly have been stunned, simply because Alexandra did not make an impression. Not any impression—whether good, bad, funny or gloomy. She seemed the epitome of unexceptional.

"List your strongest qualities." The words on the form swam before Alexandra's eyes and her heart rate increased dramatically. Her strengths? What could they possibly be? She didn't think she had any real strengths. She was neither beautiful nor clever nor athletic nor good at.... Strengths? Her eyes darted fearfully through the other questions, leaving her even more panicked. How would she answer? All she knew at that moment was that she certainly couldn't be anyone worthy of employment with the company who had requested this personal data.

Hours later, her anxiety had neither disappeared nor lessened. What were her strengths? Who was she? She had no idea whatsoever. She was what and who she needed to be in whatever environment she found herself.

That fateful day finally faded into a night of stormy blackness that gnawed at the core of her being. Who was she, really? Not who others said she was or who she should be. Who was *she*? She, who used to gaze at her own reflection in any mirror she could find, had never known the mirror of the soul.

Sleep did not come that night, as bedsheets lay twisted, curtains drawn tightly. When the unmerciful morning forced its way into her disorderly space, exhaustion taunted Alexandra with every move. Only steely willpower drove her forward in her daily routine.

Who was she? Did she—Alexandra Leigh Conwell—even want to know who she was? What good would it do to discover the answer? Was this knowledge worthwhile only so she could provide an honest answer when confronted with the next uncomfortable questionnaire? Was it really worth finding out? Or maybe the truth would be much too frightening. Painful. Even devastating.

The possibility that discovering who she was might be overwhelmingly empowering, exhilarating and life giving did not even occur to Alexandra.

So it was that day that she unwittingly passed judgment that hers was an inconsequential existence, and her contribution negligible, at best.

Body Slam

Every day sucked her deeper into the stranglehold of travel, work, responsibility for her children, angry and sometimes violent arguments with her estranged husband, and exhaustion. Besides being a hard worker, her specialized training made her a desirable and effective employee. Eighty-hour work weeks had become standard. But this was not accompanied with commensurate compensation. She staggered beneath the weight of clients and paperwork, while agency demands increasingly left her dizzy with fatigue.

Alarm at 5:00 a.m., shower, making lunches and leaving notes for all three children, grabbing coffee and out the door by 6:30. This way she avoided some of the traffic on her thirty-minute commute to the office. Her first task each day was to read through reports and agendas, giving her an updated framework for her day's appointments. First client at 8:00 a.m., last one scheduled for 7:00 p.m. Some nights she was home before the youngest two needed to be in bed; other nights she wasn't. In those instances her fourteen-year-old daughter managed all the after school responsibilities of homework, dinner, plus bedtime routines. Once the house was somewhat quiet, she spent hours tackling client reports and assessments. This was repeated five days a week, with unfinished work left for weekends.

There was absolutely no time to even consider alternative job options. Fixated on sheer survival, she was much too drained to realize that her qualifications could offer her so much more.

At ten minutes past five that morning she had a fleeting sensation of numbness in her right arm as she shampooed her hair, then dizziness as she reached for her towel. Without warning she slammed to the floor, having just stepped from the shower. Instantly she realized she couldn't move nor see anything. She tried to call out, but no sound came from her mouth. Would her children even hear her if she could call? Terror seized her mind, vaguely recognizing her near inability to think.

Her trained therapist mind went into crisis mode. Focus. Put every effort into thinking. What were her options? She wrestled her mind. Don't shut down! *Think*. Where was the phone? She always laid it on the chair next to the sink before showering. It must be there. But how would she get there? She tried to move any muscle that would cooperate and found she was able to pull herself along the floor inch by inch with her left arm. She reached the chair, felt up the leg and onto to the surface. There it was! *Thank God, I'm left-handed*, the thought.

The right side of her body was completely numb and refused to move. She still could see nothing. She couldn't see numbers on her phone, but she had programmed it to sense the imprint of her left thumb. She kept pressing where she thought the emergency call button must be. Faintly she heard the phone ringing. Laboriously she moved her arm toward her ear. She couldn't speak. Regardless of what she tried, no words came out. Over and over she called, unable to produce any sound. On the fifth call, she produced a guttural sound. The emergency dispatcher, detecting her location, promised to send an emergency team over immediately.

Enormous relief coursed through her. All she wanted was to drift into sweet oblivion, but distant recollections of her periodic first aid renewal courses began their silent chants: *keep the patient awake and conscious.*

She had no way to monitor the passage of time, but the wait seemed an eternity until paramedics arrived. The doorbell rang incessantly before her oldest daughter came out of her bedroom, wondering what the commotion was about so early in the morning. Cracking the unlocked bathroom door, she saw her mother lying motionless on the floor. She stifled a scream and ran for the front door. A moment later two paramedics bent over her. Backup was called immediately, and feverish emergency intervention began—checking vitals, then securing her onto a gurney.

She overheard the EMTs exchange a few words with her daughter. She was frantic with fear, realizing she could neither see her daughter nor communicate with her. She strained to speak, reach out, move. Nothing! She was immobilized. She simply heard words like, "husband," "emergency," "call," "hospital."

Once in the ambulance she allowed herself to rest. She was instantly hooked to IVs and all became still. Mercifully still. She would not become fully conscious again until twelve hours later. When she did, she fought to remember where she was, why she couldn't see and what had happened. She heard voices—familiar as well as unknown. She opened her parched lips.

"M..." she attempted to speak. She longed for her daughter's presence.

"Me-lis-sa," she finally whispered painstakingly.

A warm hand immediately grasped hers.

"Mom, I'm here! Don't worry." Her daughter's voice was anxious as she stroked her forehead with a trembling hand.

Nothing made sense. What had happened and why all the commotion?

Again she tried to speak, struggling to sort her thoughts into coherent patterns.

"Just rest, Mom," Melissa soothed.

It was twenty-one days—fifteen of which were spent in ICU—before she was released from the hospital after her stroke and subsequent brain surgery. Medical professionals had insisted on running a battery of tests to determine the reason for a stroke at age forty-two, and to assess future risk. After strenuous physical and speech therapy, movement in the right side of her body was laboriously restored and her speech returned. Her vision returned over time.

She worried about work daily, uncertain how long her position would be kept open for her. She desperately needed to work. Friends, family and every healthcare professional she had contact with urged her to reduce her workload.

>rr~

It was still dark when she opened the door to her office. Everything was as she'd left it, and a familiar, gnawing anxiety crept back into her soul.

Golden Grief

Her closed eyes twitch, involuntarily squinting as the early summer sun catches her round face. Within a minute, the two pools of iridescent blue flutter open. A smile creates twin dimples on her cheeks.

It's summer! Her very favorite time of year in her northern home. While most children the age of six love to frolic in the freshly fallen snow, create spectacular snow sculptures and slide down big mounds of snow—Sonya much prefers summers, including hide-and-seek with the family dog, henhouse escapades and talks with her favorite cow.

To Sonya it will be another glorious day, just like every day in the summertime. She bolts upright, feet swinging to the floor. Surprised that Daisy, the aging golden lab, isn't next to her on the floor, she turns to grab her worn stuffed doll, Greg—a rather ungainly looking character with faded thread eyes and unruly yarn hair. She slips down the narrow flight of stairs, careful not to waken her sisters and parents. She is on her way outside where she spends every waking summer moment—except during lightning storms.

Nightgown-clad and barefoot, Sonya peers out the door, searching for Daisy, but her beloved dog isn't to be seen. Confused, Sonya decides to pay Lola, the prettiest of all the laying hens in the henhouse, a visit. Still clinging to Greg, she pries the door open and croons, "Oh Lola, there you are. I almost couldn't find you!" Demure Lola waddles to the adoring child for her morning petting. This is their little ritual, just after sunrise, before the rest of the farm dwellers come to life.

Next, Sonya and Greg check in on the new litter of kittens in the barn. Nellie, the proud, longhaired mama, lifts her head curiously. It's better that Daisy isn't with her just yet, Sonya reasons. Nellie and Daisy aren't particularly good friends.

"Aww, Nellie! You're so cute!" Nellie can hardly be classified as "cute", skinny from nursing seven new kittens, but Sonya loves her dearly. The love is reciprocated. Sonya crouches beside the little family, stroking first Mama's upturned head, then, with her index finger, she gently strokes each kitten's miniature head. Enraptured, she continues this silent communication for several minutes.

"Sonya, where are you?" calls a high-pitched voice from across the farmyard. "Come here and get yourself dressed." Sonya's mother always needs to search for daughter number four.

Sonya is uneasy. She still hasn't seen Daisy. Nor are her morning rounds complete. She hasn't even spoken with the cows or goats yet. And why would she need to get dressed? She was dressed; she had her nightgown on.

It wouldn't do any harm to quickly tell Barbie good morning. She scoops Greg up, softly leaves Nellie and darts out the back of the barn. Out of the corner of one eye, she sees an unfamiliar gleam. It is the hunting rifle leaning up against the side of the barn, in the tall grass, behind an old, rusty tractor. Her breath catches sharply. Why is it there?

She turns toward the meadow. "Barbie," she whispers hoarsely, quietly. Instantly the great black and white Holstein lifts her head, turning in Sonya's direction. She knows the child well, and immediately begins ambling toward her. Though Sonya is dwarfed next to the massive creature, she has no fear. She reaches to touch her cool, wet nose, then stands on tiptoes to reach her downturned head.

"I love you, Barbie Doll," Sonya whispers, looking into Barbie's soft, brown eyes.

"Sonya!" Mother calls impatiently.

"I'll come back, Barbie Doll," she breathes, giving the black and white face a final pat.

But where could Daisy be? She runs back through the barn, then across the yard toward the two-story farmhouse.

"Oh, Sonya," Mother chides. "Your feet are a mess and you got your nightgown dirty." Sonya looks down, repentant.

"Sorry, Mother," she says guiltily, face remorseful. "I had to say..." she paused. "Where's Daisy?"

"Please wash up and go upstairs to change," Mother interrupts, then adds hastily, "and don't forget to put your nightgown in the laundry."

"Okay, Mother, but I..."

"I know! You had to see your animals. Just go now and get cleaned up," Mother turns to take another pan of round golden rolls from the piping hot oven.

Sonya complies, but she's frustrated—her

good humor squelched. Only she can't tell why. It is summer, after all.

Soon the whole family sits at the kitchen table, laden with mounds of rolls, an assortment of cheeses, jams, fruit and fresh milk. Coffee for the adults.

Sonya is troubled.

"Daddy, I can't find Daisy." Suddenly every face turns toward Daddy. He gulps more coffee, but remains silent.

The atmosphere is electric. Sonya looks from one to the other, fear gripping her young face. "Daddy, where is she?" the little girl demands.

"Honey, you know Daisy's not been well, don't you?" Daddy replies.

"No, not really. She just can't walk very well," Sonya protests, becoming increasingly anxious.

Her older sisters exude sympathy, which makes Sonya angry. Everyone knows where Daisy is, except for her.

"Honey, we had to put Daisy down," he said softly, eyes dark and sad.

"What does that mean, Daddy?"

"She was so sick I needed to..." his voice trails away. He clears his throat.

Shock burns in Sonya's blue eyes. "What, Daddy? You killed Daisy?" she blurts out, then begins to sob uncontrollably as many arms reach to envelope her. She flings them aside. She does not want them there.

Why? Why did Daddy do that? Why couldn't the vet give Daisy medicine? Her heart races, her mind fills with images of Daisy, the farmyard, her with arms thrown around the powerful golden neck. Then the rifle. No, it couldn't be!

"No, no, no!" she shrieks. "I want my Daisy!"

No person on earth can console the small child that day. Nor that entire summer. This single experience forever changes summertime for the carefree child of the outdoors.

Gutted

The room is dismally half-lit, shelves upon dusty shelves of antiquated volumes of every size line all four walls. The discolored ceiling—very high—is interrupted by a solitary moth-scarred globe light, protruding as if on a voiceless mission. The equally dreary wooden floor shows decades of foot traffic, each gash shrouding an untold story of abuse.

Muriel sits stiffly at the edge of her chair; Luther, her husband of eleven years, on an identical one, mere inches from her. Wordlessly they stare—waiting for *him*. The one who had summoned them. The reason for the requested "visit" still conspicuously unknown.

She clears her throat nervously; his eyes turn toward her, unseeing, both deeply overcome by their own raging thoughts. Why had this meeting been requested only a few weeks before graduation? Lord knew they had weighed every possible reason, always coming up empty.

The person whose office this had been for several generations of scholars is the stooped, aging, yet chillingly intimidating patriarch of their religious movement. Whether publicly or privately, he speaks only when *he* chooses to speak and only at the *exact moment* he wishes to speak. Both husband and wife are painfully aware of the level of reverence the movement's faithful have awarded this indomitable leader since long before either of them had been born.

Though neither dare voice the sinister feeling they perceive that day, they later admit to one another that they both view his power as almost cult-like in proportion.

With no warning whatsoever, the tired door explodes open, revealing the hunched dynamo. They leap to their feet simultaneously, each one's deferential "Good afternoon, Dr. Watson," stumbling over the other's. He sweeps his right hand wildly through the air, indicating they are to take their seats. They do so as if on command.

The venerated elder lowers himself gradually, seemingly painfully, into the dusty, sculpted burgundy brocade chair. It creaks under his modest weight. Deliberately he folds his hands in front of him and peers over his round glasses at the two members of the graduating class who will receive degrees from *his* prestigious institution next week. He inhales, then exhales with some effort. His mouth opens slowly, then closes. Finally, deliberately, he utters his first words.

"Thank you, Mr. and Mrs. Kellborn, for blessing me with your presence this afternoon."

Muriel winces, catching his unmistakable, condescending tone. She dares not glance in Luther's direction, fearing this will be seen as insecurity—or some other form of personal acquiescence.

Dr. E.S. Watson has served his mostly homogenous and ostensibly obedient constituency for nearly sixty years; thirteen as a minister in a local parish, and coming up on forty-seven as an academician at this highly esteemed theological university. He has paid his "ecclesiastical dues," and he rules with unrivaled steel.

It is Luther who rallies, responding with a cordial, "You're welcome. It is an honor, doctor." All that is left for Muriel is to smile and wordlessly nod her agreement—a very fitting response for the elder statesman.

The imposing, though slight form leans his chair back demonstratively, continuing to peer at the young couple before him. He is slow to continue, but when he speaks, statements, questions and assertions flow from his lips like staccato notes from Giuseppe Verdi's *La traviata.*

Muriel's head soon spins. Her heart rate increases, prompting unmistakable scarlet in her cheeks. She cringes at every highly charged, deliberate word: feminist; male leadership; uprising; order; defiant; silent; submissive.

Why, she agonizes, have she and her husband been chosen as recipients of this outburst—which clearly reflects the elder's openly flaunted and vehemently defended beliefs? Why? And why now? There is no explanation. And now his relentless barrage leaves no opportunity to regroup. It had been a trap. He had extended an invitation that could never have been declined, and now he ruled the encounter with utter sovereignty, extinguishing all hope for inner personal survival.

Reeling under the verbal torrent, both wife and husband become disoriented beyond recovery. They utter monosyllabic responses whenever demand arises; other times they can do nothing but nod in artificial agreement.

Suddenly, Dr. Watson jerks his body left to face his female guest squarely.

"Muriel, are you an angry woman?" he barks, more a dissonantly jagged statement of pre-determined certainty than an honest query.

Muriel's soul disintegrates—wishing to "do right"; knowing that no strain of "right" could survive this stifling atmosphere of interrogation.

She begins to perspire. Her knuckles gleam white under the pressure of her hand clasp.

"N-n-no ... No, Dr. Watson. I'm ... I truly am not angry ..." she hears her voice fade into ludicrous oblivion as she feels her blood pressure soaring. Silence. His penetrating glare sears into the depths of her soul. She feels the urgency to explain. Assure. Alleviate. But, words fail.

"I ..." Begging her mind to cooperate avails nothing.

"Speak up!" his sharp prod reverberates deep within herself. She fears he will see her shake.

"I'm passionate, but not angry." There! She had blurted out something reasonably articulate, but hardly accurate. Or is it true? *Am I angry?* Muriel's mind swirls into an insane whirlwind, blotting out all external light. The question ricochets in her plagued mind, willfully planted like an insidious land mine, working its debilitating terror.

His eyes narrow further, mouth pursed. Further deafening silence. Muriel is sure her pounding heartbeat is echoing through this entire musty cavern, clear for all to hear. She clamors for inner escape, as there is no hope of actual release until the captor methodically releases every selected torturous ordeal upon his prey.

"Are you?" he mutters, more subdued. "Is that what it is?" He continues to speak with chosen rhetoric and deliberate cadence, but neither hears.

Then: "We wouldn't want to lose *his* calling to your insolence, now would we?" he asks, one eyebrow raised toward her husband.

His final shot finds its target.

The two stumble from this place disoriented; desecrated; devastated. Especially she.

Just Another Court Hearing

Amber was running late. With quick movements her arms flew, brushing her long dark curls into submission. She pulled on her wool coat and leather boots. Fresh snow only proved to delay her further. She had a court hearing today, and she had spent too many hours the previous night in final preparations to be late. She was the defense attorney in a case involving a father who had lost access to his three-year-old son after an acrimonious divorce. The details of the case had left her chilled, but this morning she was confident. It was just another court hearing, she reasoned.

Amber hurried up the stairs to the grand entrance of the courthouse, clutching an armful of folders and her bulging black briefcase. She heaved the glass door open, sweeping in with a blast of freezing wind.

She glanced at the imposing clock on the wall, then strode to the security area for screening. Moments later she greeted her client, a man of about thirty. His rugged face mirrored the icy tentacles of fear she had battled that night.

"Don't worry, Ian," she soothed. "We have a strong case." Ian shook his head wordlessly. She held his eyes with a steadfast gaze. "Really. You must have faith in the justice system and in your integrity in this situation."

The judge called the courtroom to order.

Both Ian and Carolina—Ian's ex-wife, and

mother of their son—were called to testify. There were attorney statements, cross-questioning, interjections, calls to order and rulings of "admissible" or "inadmissible" evidence. Witnesses––a guardian ad litem, several child case workers and a pediatrician—were called to the stand, with statements that defended or defamed either of the two parents.

This was the first time in Amber's career that she was defending a parent who had had a close relationship with his child, but had subsequently been eliminated from that child's life. Today the judge would rule regarding Ian's suitability to be part of his son's life. A discussion, which should have come down *only* to the "best interest of the child," quickly escalated to a verbal tug-of-war with dizzying accusations, assertions and assumptions.

The attorney representing Carolina was calculated. Amber was repeatedly forced to regroup, responding to the staggering frequency with which his tactics changed. In all her years of practice she had never experienced what she considered such flagrant violation of family law. Repeatedly she called into question the opposing counsel's twisting of legal statements. Sometimes the judge ruled in her favor; other times not. It was impossible to determining the outcome.

After fifty-seven minutes, the judge announced a recess, calling them to reconvene in one hour. Amber exhaled, silently staring ahead for a moment. She turned to her client after a swift mental recalibration. "Shall we step into the hallway?"

Ian rose with obvious fatigue. Worry had crept

back into his hazel eyes, dejection visible in his demeanor. Amber leaned to speak into his ear, "Ian, I need you to square your shoulders and look as confident as you can until we reach a place where we can speak in private." He understood and they walked out together—past the ex-wife, her family members and opposing counsel.

While they ate their tuna fish salad slapped between two slices of stale rye bread in the courthouse cafeteria, Amber and Ian reviewed statements, reinforced strategy and agreed on which claims from the other side were the most egregious, and therefore in definite need of challenging. Keeping the distraught father on task was daunting. She listened with compassion as he rehearsed the times he'd been misquoted, blamed, and blatantly lied about in the past hour. He was deeply wounded.

"Ms. Amber, I just couldn't take it when he cried—his little arms stretched to me screaming, 'please don't go!'" he blurted out, referring to the child.

Her face softened; her words comforted.

"Did you know that Carolina has said some pretty vile things about my mother, too?"

Amber paused, faltering slightly. "No, I didn't know that." A cold wind whistled through her bones.

When they again took their seats in the courtroom, Amber was certain that Ian was in a better space. She would intensify her focus, apply her strategies and present the closing arguments with precision. The opposing counsel changed his demeanor, barked statements, demanded "justice" and insisted on complete removal of the child from his father.

When it was her turn to speak, Amber was rational and methodical. And she was forceful. All her arguments were based solidly on research, the law and what *she* regarded to be undeniably in the "best interest of the child."

A moment later the judge's gavel fell: full custody to the mother, with two hours of supervised visitation to the father weekly. Amber reeled; Ian gasped. They collected their papers while the exuberant maternal party exited the courtroom with raucous laughter and congratulatory high fives.

As they turned towards the door, a tall, simply dressed older woman approached them. Ian reached to give her a hug, then turned to introduce her to Amber as his mother. Amber smiled, assuring her that this was *not* the end of their fight. Ian's mother thanked her with a genuine handshake.

Later, in the safety of her twenty-seventh floor condo, Amber sank into her overstuffed chair in front of the fire. Her body shook—cold, in spite of the warm, dancing flames. Her face was somber, her eyes moist. Her hand slowly caressed the emerald suede of the armrest. *I love this chair. I can't believe it's one of the only pieces that once belonged to her that I got,* she agonized. *And to think, I even had to fight to get this when she died.*

That night, her thoughts drifted back to another time and another city where she, too, had "lost" a loving grandmother to the system which had ruled in an alienator's favor, in just another court hearing.

Hearing Voices

~~~

"Are you hearing voices, Ms. Crayfield?" he asks Maggie with pompous aloofness.

Shit, don't we all? Maggie thinks amusedly to herself. She turns slightly to face the overzealous professional squarely. "Voices? You mean actual voices in my head?" Maggie responds with her own brand of unflappable cleverness.

The young, self-assured psychiatrist narrows his eyes, and shoots back with steely precision, "Yes, ma'am. What other voices might you be hearing?"

Maggie's gaze does not falter. Oh, she hears voices alright. Her mind rattles off dozens of responses she could give him:

"Don't do that, sweetheart. You're not strong enough to lift that."

"Come back here, you idiot. Your place is not on that stage. That's for people with real talent."

"Here! Get this done before I'm back in the office tomorrow at 7 a.m."

"You're absolutely wrong about that! Where do you get your ideas anyway?"

"Get out of here. I don't have time for you."

"Ah, right. You're the new professor. I'll give you two weeks with that class before you're in a mental hospital."

She could have kept going. The voices rattle on and on. But not voices caused by an unstable mental condition. She is very certain about that.

She brings herself back to the present

effortlessly. "I'm not sure you'd like for me to answer that, Dr...," she begins with a condescending smile, squinting at the opulent bronze name plaque resting obtrusively between her and "..., Dr. Emerson."

She can play this game. She has learned to unnerve psychiatrists, therapists, counselors, ministers—basically anyone who might consider themselves as superior in training or insight. It is just a matter of time. Her wit is sharp, her tongue quick. At this point, she has no option but to outsmart them.

"Oh yes, Ms. Crayfield. I would love for you to answer that question," Dr. Emerson bears on, suggesting he relishes anything that might develop into a cat-and-mouse chase. Maggie's eyes keep their steady hold on the face before her. She shakes her head almost imperceptibly.

Everyone thinks there is something wrong with her. New appointments keep being made for her with an ever-rotating flurry of mental, psychological and spiritual authorities—all of who are to address, in some way, the reality in which she finds herself. Or rather, the mental state they perceive her to be in.

"Certainly you can't believe that! It's blasphemy!"

"Look here, love. We've registered you for this really helpful retreat."

"That happened decades ago. You shouldn't blame others forever."

"Can't you see it? That's entirely unhealthy."

"What I hear in my head, Dr. Emerson, are the questions you are asking me. In fact, you sound like a recording of the last therapist who was thrust upon me like a shoe two sizes too small," she replies with mocking sweetness. Her voice does not match the hostility in her eyes. But Dr. Emerson seems not to focus on her eyes, rather continues to address merely the words she chooses to utter, and his dissatisfaction with those words.

Maggie is a brilliant, intuitive idealist who sees life through lenses few understand. She rarely fits patterns, therefore creating mistrust inadvertently.

"There must be some reason your sister referred you to my practice, Ms. Crayfield. Are you telling me that she misrepresented your condition?"

"I'm not sure which condition you're talking about, doctor."

"Hearing voices, Maggie." He nearly spits out her given name. "You are hearing voices, telling you to do things," he snarls, almost demanding she agree with his professional assessment.

Maggie sighs, focuses her eyes on the wall behind this intrusion and waits for yet another person to add to the voices she already carries with her. Deciding for her and about her. Telling her what to do. If it weren't so sickeningly monotonous and energy-zapping, she might find it amusing.

A string of formless characters parade like a line of actors in a mock audition for a drama lacking any coherence.

"That color makes your skin look like dead fish."

"All you need is a few drinks to get over that inhibition."

"I'll have to ask you to move. This seat is reserved for donors to the agency."

"As the person in authority, I will have to ask you to comply with the rules."

"I'm not asking you—I'm telling you. Don't ever contact me again."

Maggie can hear Dr. Emerson's voice droning on. Because she would just as soon not hear what he had to say, she interjects a question of her own:

"And what, in your clinical opinion, is a suitable solution to the condition you imagine me having?"

He stops short. Dumbfounded. "I...," his voice fades. His forehead wrinkles slightly, and he appears to struggle to regain his train of thought. "Well," he continues, "first you need to tell me more about yourself."

Before he can add any further qualifiers, she proceeds.

"I'm five feet, six and a half inches tall."

"I have an apartment in Manhattan as well as a house in the hills of North Carolina."

"I'm a professor of English literature—going on eight years at New York University."

"I'm a hobby runner, sculptor and kayaker."

"I love theater, fire pits and eating chocolate pudding."

Then she pauses a brief moment, reveling in his astonished facial expression.

"Anything else you'd like to know about me, Dr. Emerson?" she asks, rising from her chair, striding to the door.

"Ms. Crayfield, stop. Maggie, please sit down." He fumbles, grating his chair backward along the ancient wooden floor slats beneath. "You cannot simply walk out of here. You are in danger..."

But, "Ms. Crayfield" stops him right there. With one hand on the door handle, she says, "That's where you're wrong, Dr. Emerson. I can, and I will." Then she adds with quiet, unmistakable authority, "Please save your voice for an unwitting soul who, regrettably, will allow you to add your voice to the myriad of other voices in their head."

Taffeta Sailor

Clattering pans and clacking machines. Mounds of dough transformed into shapely trees, stars, bells and reindeer. Pungent aromas coming from heaps of golden cookies. Sluggishly blinking Christmas tree lights. Colliding tunes from adjacent rooms as one plays the flute, another the clarinet, yet another the viola. Every available surface scattered with fabric odds and ends, matching ribbon, piping and lace being fashioned into delicate Christmas outfits for festive occasions. It was as if her entire world bustled in awestruck expectancy of the Christmas season.

But it really wasn't Christmas Day itself that Sage, youngest of four, brimmed in anticipation of. It wasn't the thought of staying up late to open gifts on Christmas Eve (gifts were *never* delayed until Christmas morning), nor was it the crisp, new dress or lilting Christmas carols, not even the bounteous feast at Granny's house that brought Sage the greatest joy. One splendid event held the most magic of all. It was the annual school Christmas program that enraptured her little soul.

Ever since she could walk, Sage had bobbed alongside her mother and father and three older sisters to crowd into the schoolhouse where glitter, excited laughter and bright-eyed wonder were everywhere. This was Christmas program night—the plain school-room transformed into a mystical, wondrous paradise when all the lights were dimmed. All, that is, except those on the magnificent Christmas tree in the front of the room and the faint lights, precariously strung up to illuminate the makeshift stage.

There were always dramatic presentations at these concerts—*always*. Sage's eyes shone. She could barely wait to be one of the chosen few who acted out whichever story the teacher chose for that year. She imagined herself there on stage, every year. If only she were old enough to sit in one of the desks for the big school children. But even more important, if she were only old enough to be part of this rapturous night.

Then suddenly it happened. She was old enough. She was one of the *big* kids!

Now it was already her second year to be able to participate. Her little heart nearly burst. This year she would be a sailor who would steer one of the "three ships" as they sailed in on Christmas Day, with accompanying pompous music underscoring the drama. Her slight frame bounced up the aisle to take her place with the actors, many guests already seated on wobbly chairs placed close together.

Today her Christmas outfit was more splendid than ever. Her mother had made what to Sage was an exquisite dress in deep blue taffeta. It swished whenever she moved, her dark eyes sparkling with pleasure. Her shoulders shivered with delight.

"Where are you off to in such a hurry, little miss?" a gruff voice called from one of the collapsible chairs in the third row. Startled, Sage turned her head sharply to see bearded Mr. Williams, the community letter carrier, who always looked as if he needed a haircut and a new pair of shoes.

"I...I..." her high-pitched voice faltered.

"Speak up, child!" he rumbled.

Sage just wanted to get up to the stage, close to where *her ship* stood in the harbor. She turned to run, but he suddenly reached out and grabbed her tiny, white wrist.

"I asked you something. It's rude not to answer," he chided.

Trying to wriggle free, she blurted out, "I'm going to my ship."

The scruffy man looked bemused. "*Your* ship?" he scoffed.

"Yes, my ship," she insisted with a voice that would have accompanied two hands on her hips, had her right hand been free. "Now let me go," she blurted with some force. "Please", she added, wishing to give her request strength.

"What will you do with *your* ship?" he sneered.

"I'm a sailor and I'm going to sail the ship into the harbor," she explained with growing impatience. "I have to go."

His eyes narrowed and he gripped her wrist even more tightly. She flinched.

"A *girl* can't be a sailor," he snarled, eyes darkening.

Her forehead wrinkled and her eyes flashed.

"Uh-huh, they can, too," she countered bravely, nodding her head up and down fiercely.

He leaned close. Sage pulled back from his whiskery face. "Girls are stupid. They are weak and can't do important things like sailing ships," he rasped. "Look at you! You can't sail a ship in *that* dress!"

The miniature sailor was about to cry when she saw a familiar shape taking the chair next to Mr. Williams in the darkness that enveloped the suddenly threatening schoolroom.

"Good evening, Postman Williams," the familiar voice flowed into the darkness, causing the icicle hold on Sage's wrist to melt instantly. Her daddy looked up at her, "Go on now, Little Miss Sailor. Do a great job steering that ship tonight."

That deep caramel voice always brought peace to her heart and resolve to every task. Sage danced the final few feet up to the stage, which felt as comfortable to her as the kitchen table heaped high with cookies to frost. Her daddy was right. *He* knew that she was good enough, smart enough and strong enough to be a sailor. She smoothed the dark blue taffeta, then rubbed her right wrist a little. The sparkle returned to her eyes as she took her place on the bridge of *her* ship.

Season's Pleadings

It was an enchanting scene. The elaborate building was adorned with shimmering lights, sparkling stars, dangling shapes, all glowing like a thousand stars against the velvety blackness of the winter night. She sat for a moment, taking in both the brilliance of the scene and the wonder of her good fortune to be there at that very moment. Anticipating what had seemed impossible.

Georgia breathed deeply, then stepped from her car into the brisk evening, shivering slightly as she approached the glamorous sight. To her utter astonishment, she had been invited to join family members at a Christmas extravaganza at this astounding location—a community center in the upscale, gated neighborhood in which her daughter, son-in-law and four-year-old granddaughter lived.

Though Georgia lived in the same city, it had been nearly thirteen months since she had last been granted entrance to this property. At that time she'd been invited to celebrate her son-in-law's medical school graduation. There had been no contact since then. No calls returned, no emails responded to, no gifts sent, no time shared with any of them. Not even on holidays or birthdays.

Tonight Georgia would see her family. Breathing a "thank you" wordlessly, she heaved the etched glass door open and strode in. Removing her leather gloves, she scanned the crowd for one of those three familiar faces. As she checked her coat, a familiar voice rang out. Then two tiny arms wrapped around her waist.

"Gram!" the voice cried. "You came!"

Georgia turned quickly, dropping to a crouch next to an impressive, intricately handcrafted crèche. Eyes closed momentarily, she held the little one, stroking her flaxen hair.

"Oh, Emma Jo," was all she whispered. Then, as quickly as they had embraced, Georgia held the child at arm's length to look into her hazel eyes. The little girl's eyes reflected wonder, almost as if she hardly dared believe it was true.

"Aren't you a big girl by now," Georgia beamed. How painfully she had missed the little one.

Then began the happy chatter.

"Gram, did you know that I'm in preschool?"

"Do you know that I'm taking flute lessons?"

"My mommy baked a hundred Christmas cookies."

"Gram, we have a new puppy. Her name is Simone."

Reunited at last, the two did not hide their delight. Quite quickly, they were joined by Emma Jo's mother and father. Georgia's willowy daughter, Debra, was regal in an elegant silk gown, diamonds sparkling at every turn of her head of dark curls.

"Hello, dear," Georgia exclaimed as she pulled Debra close for a moment. Little warmth accompanied the reciprocated hug.

"Hi, Mom," Debra returned, smiling faintly.

Georgia turned to her distinguished, boyishly handsome son-in-law. "And a very good evening to you, doctor. Good to see you," she smiled. Nathan kept his distance, but acknowledged her with a formal handshake.

Emma Jo's endearing vibrancy began to melt the ice around the edges of the initially stilted adult interactions. She bounced from friend to friend as Debra introduced her mother to friends and colleagues. Conversation flowed as toasts were made, silver trays laden with hors d'oeuvres were served and music was performed.

Emma Jo found her Gram repeatedly, sharing stories, offering hugs, exchanging attentive glances. At one point Emma Jo reached her arms up, "Please pick me up, Gram."

Georgia set her empty champagne glass down, wondering whether she could still lift the lanky four-year-old. Indeed she could—barely—and the child enveloped her grandmother with an adoring hug.

"I love you, Gram," she whispered from her tight embrace.

"Emma J, I love you so much, too," Georgia replied.

Emma Jo giggled, "Emma J! I like it when you call me that."

Georgia smiled, bittersweetness flooding her soul.

"Gram, I wish I could come to your house."

Tears sprang to Georgia's eyes. She, too, wished nothing more, but there was a hostile history between herself and Emma Jo's parents.

"Emma J," she began. "Never, never forget how much Gram loves you!"

The child released the grip on her Gram's neck enough to be inches from her face.

"Why can't I come see you, Gram?" Her eyes were sorrowful. Agonizing. Hopeless.

Georgia paused only briefly. "Sweet Emma J, we must be brave. We must pray. We must wait until Mommy and Daddy think it's a good idea for you to come." She grasped for some wisp of hope. "Can you do that, sweetheart?"

"No," she wailed in hushed tones, embracing her Gram again. "No, Gram. I don't want to wait. I want to come now."

Georgia mustered all her emotional faculties, trying with all her might to craft words of hope, love, courage and joy for her small granddaughter. Evidently it sufficed, for the little one wiggled back to the floor and ran to play.

Through enormous effort, Georgia resumed her festive conversation with other guests, but her heart was broken. Every time Emma Jo would come for a hug or to exchange a few words, Georgia would focus on the small treasure.

Then it came time to go. Georgia searched out Debra and Nathan, expressed her gratitude, wished them a Merry Christmas, then bent to say goodbye to Emma Jo. The child clung to her neck and would not let go.

"No, Gram! Don't go!" she whimpered. "Please, don't go."

Georgia did her best to console her, aware that her words rang hollow.

Suddenly a scream pierced the controlled, stately environment. "I don't want you to go," Emma Jo shrieked in desperation. Every head turned with distanced disdain to observe the disorderly scene.

Debra and Nathan acted quickly, pulling Emma Jo from her grandmother and silencing her with steely eyes and an abrupt reprimand. Choking on her tears she gave in.

Georgia turned to go. Numb. She had no recollection of how she left that opulent scene—the lights now mocking. Garish. Hypocritical.

Now Georgia sat in her car in silence. Anguished. Destroyed.

9 a.m. Monday

>ᴧ~

Tanya rubbed her belly with her left hand, her right hand clutching the strap of a faded backpack weighted with books, a tablet and a bottle of water. She felt the tiny girl kicking within her, responding to her caress. She walked more slowly than usual; she was seven months pregnant.

Classmates around the room shouted greetings and her best friend whispered in her ear, "Hey, Tan! How ya feelin'?" The mother-to-be sank wearily into a chair at one of the classroom tables.

"I'm okay," she told Mercedes, breathing heavily as she unpacked what she would need for the class. She didn't want to tell her best friend the truth.

Tanya didn't know the speaker that day, but she introduced herself as Maria, a local life coach and therapist. Tanya was ready to shut her out, as she didn't need any coaching and most surely *didn't* need a shrink. She took a long sip from her water bottle. It was important to stay hydrated, her gynecologist had insisted.

This whole pregnancy thing was turning out to be an education in and of itself, but not always in a good way. She had thought there was nothing much to it, really. But, then she had begun feeling sick in the mornings, and Scottie—her boyfriend—would get mad. He didn't get it that she didn't feel like having sex when she was ready to throw up. She rolled her eyes in disdain when he whined. Plus, she began talking more about the baby than about him. That made him really mad. So he hit her—more than usual. She had been sure he would calm down once her belly started to grow, but that had seemed to aggravate him even more. She would try to twist her body away from him when she suspected a blow, trying to shield the baby. It was terrifying. And exhausting.

Last night Tanya had slept almost not at all. Scottie hadn't been home when she had gone to bed, so she worried about him. He also hadn't called—which wasn't unusual. Then, at 2:30 a.m. she finally heard him in the parking lot of her apartment. He wasn't alone and he was yelling at whoever was with him. Fear gripped her. She lay in bed, rigid, hoping he wouldn't do anything stupid. Voice decibels rose and she could understand every word. She was sure curtains were being pulled back ever so slightly by neighbors always trigger happy about calling the cops. She froze. What should she do? The only door in the apartment led to the parking lot where Scottie was cussing and threatening someone. She could tell he was either drunk or high. She reached for her cell phone. But whom would she call? Now she wished she'd stayed over at Mercedes' after their shopping spree. Mercedes, already seventeen—a whole year older than Tanya—had warned her that Scottie was "up to no good". Of course Tanya had argued that *she* knew Scottie better than anyone. After all, he was her boo. But now she was beside herself.

Tanya heard Scottie climbing the stairs and she was sure she would pass out. She felt like throwing up, too. She quickly slipped into the bathroom and locked the door.

The apartment door flew open and Scottie stormed in. He yelled obscenities, looking for her, demanding to know where she was. She wrestled to keep from screaming in panic, desperate to remain calm. Finally, she hoarsely called out that she had needed to use the restroom and would be out in a minute.

"Get yourself outta there. Now!" he barked. He wasn't messin', she thought.

She quickly opened the door, putting on her most soothing voice, all the while nearly overcome with fear. He certainly was on something—what, exactly, she didn't know. She prayed, even though she never prayed. She was desperate.

"Absolutely nothing you do or say gives your partner the right to cuss you out or hurt you in any way." Those words snapped her out of her mental turmoil. It was Maria.

"Wait...what?" she said without thinking, her hand unintentionally half-raised. All eyes turned toward her. Embarrassed, she tried to brush it off nonchalantly. "Oh, never mind. I just thought I'd misunderstood something, but..." her voice trailed off while tears flooded her eyes.

"Go on," Maria encouraged. "You can ask any question."

She paused uneasily. Silence. One of the guys in the front row, a boy big enough to be a football player, turned around in his seat and urged, "Yeah, Tan. We gotcho back. Go!"

"What'd you say about a partner cussin' or beatin' on you?" Tanya asked.

"There is nothing that makes it okay for anyone to either verbally or physically attack you," Maria said.

Confusion clouded Tanya's face. Hurt filled her eyes. Twice she tried to speak, but she could say nothing.

Maria waited, then said, "Does that make sense?"

"But, but..." Tanya struggled with words, and to keep her emotions in check. "But that's how he lets me know he loves me. Ya know? He just wants me to do right. Be in line. Ya know?"

Silence.

After briefly pondering, Maria said, "Love, kindness, protection and support are how a great partner will show you he loves you."

Tanya stared. A million thoughts collided in her brain. Her heart beat rapidly. Instinctively she rubbed her belly, calming the little one within her.

"But..." she ventured again. Silence. She lifted her eyes. "Are you sure?" Pause. "Sure cussin' and beatin' don't do that? I know he means well."

Maria said simply, "That's right. Cussing and beating destroys you. You deserve respect. Protection. Love. To be treated as an equal."

Tanya's hand trembled, but kept circling her belly. Finally, "Ms. Maria, I never knew that. I've had boyfriends since I was twelve, and I never knew that."

A hush fell over the room.

"You deserve better, Tanya."

Darkness

>⟋⟍

Her entire body shook. Her breath came in short, wheezing spasms. Shiver after shiver ran over her already cold body. *It feels like a freezer in here,* she thought. Mechanically she guided her rusty car toward home, past one familiar landmark and another.

Never before had she felt so diminished. So crushed. Like her soul had simply been trampled on. *Never.* She had suffered all kinds of humiliation, scorn and danger before—but this? What had just occurred defied comprehension.

As she waited for a traffic light to turn green, she leaned her head against the window. She prayed the light would stay red forever, fearing she was too destroyed to go on. But she knew she needed to continue driving. She needed to be home. Mercifully the day at work had come to an end. The violent parking lot encounter was behind her and—she was still breathing. Yes, still breathing and moving. Violated. Bruised. Horrified. But somehow, still alive—a startling discovery. An involuntary chuckle escaped past her downturned lips.

Robotically she lifted her right foot from the brake when the light turned. The car hesitated slightly—just enough to shoot fear into her battered heart. No. It could *not* die again. She couldn't afford another repair bill, nor could she miss one more day of work. She couldn't even miss another second of work for that matter. Her heart rate quickened, her mind propelling her thoughts towards two small, wide-eyed faces. Kitt and Damien. Her two gems. The only ones who could still make her smile. Her sole reason for carrying on. They depended on her to at least put some noodles on the table each night. She must not fail. She dared *never* miss work again. Already she was past due on the electric bill and every night she feared coming home to find her shack of a house dark and cold. Colder than it already was.

After the barely decipherable hiccup, the car recovered, as if it had caught a stern warning glance from a rigid schoolmaster. It groaned and creaked, one mile after another. *Nearly there*, she voicelessly nudged it forward. She dared not relive the horror of what had happened moments earlier in the parking lot. Not now. Just *focus*.

She drove on, heart in her throat, dreading the possibility that her lowly hovel might be pitch black and cold when she arrived. She'd made arrangements with the mother of her school-aged babysitter so Kitt and Damien could at least temporarily find refuge with them should power to her home be cut. Rounding the final the corner, she gasped—*darkness*. Or wait—was there a faint pencil line of light seeping from the far side of the tiny structure? Indeed there was. Though it cast only an anemic glow onto the white snow, it was as if she had seen the portals of heaven. She pulled herself from the barely warmed car, exhaled slowly, tilted her head back ever so briefly. With eyes closed, she wordlessly breathed a grateful sigh into the crackling night air.

Instinctively she pulled her scarf up to shield her face from the onslaught of icy air. In a few steps she blew in the front door, threatening to extinguish the timid flames in the open fireplace. As long as the wood supply would last, she had resolved to use the bare minimum of electrical kilowatts.

The four arms that instantly encircled her and the squeals of delight that ignited the sparse living space fueled her flagging spirit. At once her face shone, liberally bestowing whatever light she still possessed onto her beloved treasures. For a moment all else dissolved into the sound and sight of love and belonging. The gaunt young girl who watched over the little ones pulled on her outerwear and disappeared with a faint wave out the door and into the vehicle that had appeared in the driveway moments earlier.

The next hour there was laughter, tumbling, singing and cuddling, requiring great amounts of determination to push through her growing discomfort. The spindly toddlers, soon exhausted, were hurriedly dressed in night clothing much too big for them, then heaped with blankets and threadbare towels—weapons to combat the encroaching cold that seeped in all around them. As the embers sputtered with finality, deprived of replenishment, she was again alone with her thoughts.

Hands on the narrow armrests, she allowed her body to sink slowly into the creaking wooden rocker that threatened to splinter into a thousand pieces should it become unwilling to bear her weight. Searing pain sliced through her body, torturous thoughts thrust themselves upon her like an aggressor subduing his victim. Her eyelids tightly closed against the memory of her devastating violation. Her soul was dark. Cold. Barren. Numb and unfeeling. *Nothing can change this,* she conceded inwardly. The only sources of light and warmth that remained were now asleep beneath mounds of bedclothes. *If I didn't have them,* she reasoned, *there would truly be no point in continuing. It would make no sense to go through all of this just for me.*

Her face turned. There they were. So she would stay. For them. She could bear the horror, the cold, the complete absence of light, knowing they would once again awaken before dawn to fill her world with light. In the recesses of her soul, she knew that using two innocent children as her only motivation to live was too much weight to place onto their fledgling lives, but she had neither the strength nor the understanding to change it. Her head dropped. She pulled the old knitted throw over herself and sat. Motionless.

Easter's Lavender

She ran her tiny hand slowly over the gleaming fabric, fingering the lace and delicate buttons. It was her favorite color. *Lavender*. Already she imagined how she would twirl, wide skirt flying, her buckled white patent shoes clicking as she danced. Would her friends also have special Easter dresses when they met in their Sunday School class for eight-year-olds? Surely hers would be the most exquisite.

She jumped as she felt the hand rest on her shoulder, the deep voice whispering, "Show me how pretty you are, sugar." Her body stiffened. Her heart began racing so furiously that every part of her body pulsated. He never called her "sugar" except when he came to call on her—in her bedroom, door closed off from the rest of the family.

"C'mon. Show your daddy a good time, now, sugar. You know I'll give you extra Easter eggs."

Her head swam. Her eyes refused to see. She couldn't move. Not a muscle. His hand grasped her shoulder more firmly and turned her to face him. Her head dropped to her chest. She could not bear to look at him.

Tears stung her tightly closed eyes. She forced her mind to take her to the meadow. The one where she played with her cousin every summer in the warm sun. Both laughing. Tumbling into the tall grasses with the pungent aroma of lavender in bloom. She loved the color lavender. It was a happy, safe color. A warm, carefree color.

She refused to see, feel and think about what her hands were forced to do, his body thrust upon her. Every time the same. She shut out the sensation of lying on her very own bed. Where she slept at night. *No, no!* She was lying in the prairie grasses on a warm summer day. Clouds caressed her mind. She refused to hear the sounds next to her face, choosing rather the cawing of birds overhead. She remembered only the scent of flowers which masked the acrid stench that accompanied these episodes. She was safe. All was peaceful. The scene serene.

"Sugar?" the voice called her away from the safety of the meadow. "What's wrong with you? Get cleaned up and dressed for breakfast right now. We've got to read the Easter story before we head to church."

Feeling returned to her body one tingling limb at a time. The precariously rotating prison, once more her taunting bedroom. Her heart was cold. She stifled a sob.

"You've got to hurry, Grace." Her daddy's voice was suddenly gruff and he tugged at her arm with his massive hand. "Don't be late or your mother will ask what took you so long."

She thought they had Easter bread that morning, but she couldn't remember. Somehow she had struggled painfully into her new outfit and wiggled into her socks and shoes. Alone. She didn't recall how.

"Hey, baby, here's your church dress for Easter. Get up now so we won't be late."

The small child stirred in her sleep, reminding her of who she once had been. She stroked the curly head of hair and kissed the soft cheek. "C'mon. I'm fixin' eggs and biscuits. I know you'll want some."

Together the two hurried into the stately red brick building, immediately surrounded by other giggling girls who quickly spirited the little one away to children's church. Mama looked on proudly. *My baby loves lavender too*, she smiled to herself, admiring her ruffly little princess. *Just like her Mama.* She smoothed her suit—also lavender.

She turned to walk into the sanctuary where others were already gathered and singing joyously. It was Easter Sunday—the most inspiring of all religious celebrations. She turned to the stained glass windows, letting a single shaft of golden light envelop her, eyes becoming moist at the wonder of the moment. Truly her life had been transformed. She had found stability, peace and safety.

She sang enthusiastically and repeated prayers reverently. Everything contributed to the soothing grace in which she now lived. All was well. Her eyes closed in gratitude.

"I know many people have experienced hard things in life." The minister's voice broke into her serenity. "Some have lost loved ones, others have battled debilitating illnesses. Still others have struggled with limited finances. But *this* is why we celebrate Easter. This single event changes everything."

Grace smiled in agreement.

"There are people who've experienced unspeakable pain. Maybe in childhood. Maybe as an adult."

Her body stiffened and then trembled. Dizziness swept over her. She recognized this feeling. Immediately her mind flew to the meadow.

"Some of you have been beaten, humiliated and abused. Some even sexually abused."

She fought to retain control over her body, mind and voice. She wanted to scream, *No! No! Stop those words!* Better still, she needed to run and hide. Hide *somewhere*. How did he know? Who else knew?

"Today we want to pray for anyone who has been sexually abused as a child."

She gasped, instinctively clapping a hand over her mouth to stifle any sound. If she didn't, she felt certain that she would utter a most terrifying cry— definitely not fit for the house of God. *Oh Lord have mercy*, was all her mind repeated.

"If you've been sexually abused as a child, I want you to raise your hand now so we can pray for you."

The words seemed as if they were emerging out of a vast cavern. Heartless, mocking words. She wrestled to suppress the searing pain. Around her she saw hand after hand lifting, wrenching sobs engulfing poor, harrowed souls. Like her! The hand not over her mouth remained resolutely in her lap. Even the meadow betrayed her; held no refuge.

Confusion gripped her soul. Where was she? She had thought this was her safe place. But this? *This* was not safety.

Later she couldn't remember whether or not she and her baby girl had eaten Easter bread that year. But they had both worn lavender.

Paints, Palettes and Pathos

Quickly she grabs the faded leather bag containing her supplies and peers in: a small assortment of natural brushes, tubes of paint, a color palette, a lightweight painting smock, a purse-sized package of paper towelettes and two small clear jars to fill with water when on-site. She speaks in low tones to two identical cocker spaniels, Suds and Spuds, lets them outside and then back in, and feeds them their much-anticipated evening meal.

Angeline glances at the round stainless steel clock above her kitchen table. She's late! She reaches for her loosely fitting linen jacket to later throw on over her calf-length, bold floral sundress when night falls. Inwardly cross, she gets in her car and makes her way across town, blaming the unscheduled end-of-the-day office meeting for running late. But her frustration soon dissipates and her face brightens as she explodes into the expansive studio.

"Angeline!" The cries come from every corner of the room, all eyes focusing on the tall, striking woman who has just breezed in. Angeline removes her sunglasses, revealing dark eyes that flash intense passion, pushes unruly black curls away from her round face, and holds her arms out wide. She stops short for one brief moment. "Hey, you!" she returns enthusiastically, striding forward to embrace every member of her tight-knit painting clique. "You know I love y'all more than life itself!" she says, bestowing her words effusively on anyone and everyone within earshot.

An outsider might recoil at Angeline's noisily vivacious personality, but every person here adores her. While the group has no designated leader— meeting every week simply for the joy of painting and to share new projects, techniques and insights— Angeline is the one who brings elevated motivation, activity and decibel levels. She is central. *Key.*

Tonight the music reflects the Latin American group members' preference. Salsa, samba and merengue underscore their passion as the eleven unpack painting equipment, working with the same invisible drive embodied in the music. Each artist is positioned at one of two butcher-block tables, bending over paper, paints and palettes. Effortlessly they create, moving to inspect one another's evolving work and commenting on color, texture and motif. Dance, music and style are interwoven like various mediums in a mesmerizing masterpiece.

There is nothing that brings Angeline more joy than art. Nothing. Anywhere. She loves her demanding career as a securities lawyer. She is unselfishly devoted to her three much younger half-sisters, all of them essentially deserted when her stepfather suddenly moved her mother and himself to a remote commune in Ecuador. She dotes endlessly on the spaniel duo, who bring laughter at all hours, day or night. But art—all types of art, really, but specifically the never-ending possibilities of watercolor—delight her heart. Here she can express her passion for beauty, movement and brilliance. Simply sharing the same space with other equally ignited creatives brings peace to her soul.

"You're quite the little artist," the oldest among them breathes at Angeline's neck. Carlos could be her grandfather, has painted since he was eight, and is undeniably her favorite of all. She tilts her head to one side, straightens and surveys her unfolding splashes of color. She reciprocates Carlos' warmth with a genuine, "Thank you, love!"

"...quite the little artist." The words swirl in Angeline's mind as she turns back to her work. Deep within, her stomach knots. Her forehead wrinkles and she can't explain her sudden sense of nausea. Why? One minute earlier she had danced the merengue with Jovan–a sultry, smooth dancer, who invariably causes her face to flush and heart rate to increase. Maybe that dance had been too much, given her empty stomach, she reasons. She hadn't had dinner.

The feelings persist. *"...quite the little artist."* Her mind mechanically tosses the phrase round and round, like the dangling seats on a Ferris wheel at a country fair. Where had she heard these words before and why do they just upset her so? The smile vanishes from her face, perspiration gleams on her forehead and the strokes of her brush dance a furious dance all their own. It is so confusing. Her head reels. *"...quite the little artist."* Haunting. Taunting. Troubling.

Lightheaded, her mind suddenly becomes the backdrop for a theater production, presenting a cast of two. Only two. A small dark-haired girl of about three, a woman who looks like the adult version of the three-year-old, both stand before a large easel. Woman and child have brushes in their hands, dipping them into small jars of oil paints which stand in an orderly line like toy soldiers in bright uniform. The canvas on the wooden structure, low enough for the child to reach easily, is already filled with vibrant color. Woman and child laugh and banter, chase each other playfully, embrace frequently.

Angeline catches her breath. She knows this scene. She's been in it. This is she and her mother in carefree times. In sync. In the moment. It is before her stepfather came to play a suppressive role in the family and before the three babies—as her mother called her sisters—were born. Mother had always applauded her artistic ability whenever they painted. It had been she who often enthused, "You're quite the little artist."

"Ange, darling, are you alright?" It is Carlos, inches from her. He has observed the sudden change in her demeanor, sensing her agitation. Angeline does not hear him, involuntarily lets out a piercing cry, burying her face in her hands. She trembles violently.

"No, no, no!" she shrieks. "He took her away! She would never have left us. Never!" Immediately Carlos wraps his bare, brown arms around her, holding her to his chest. Her sobs and utter despair dominate every level of her existence. She is unaware of the other nine, crowding around. Reaching. Consoling.

Engulfed in anguish. Sinking. Forsaken. Shattered.

Ninety-Nine

ᕗ

"Thirteen; forty-five; seventy-one; ninety-nine!" she bellowed as she jostled through the kitchen door, flinging her backpack, tied together running shoes and disheveled jacket onto the floor beside the kitchen counter. Kate's eyes gleamed, her face reflecting innocent pleasure at her self-assessed brilliant diversionary tactic. Her mother turned from her culinary task, faint exasperation turning quickly to a good-natured expression of amusement at her daughter's endless tricks.

Nine-year-old Kate had a brain that continually worked overtime concocting games, puzzles, riddles, and anything else to cause levity. This particular trick was far from new. Kate delighted in shouting out random numbers, trying to confuse her mother as she counted out teaspoons, tablespoons, cups, drops or pinches of salt, sugar, baking soda, flour—basically anything used in baking. Kate dissolved in laughter. She never tired of this game.

"Ah, my dear," chuckled her mother. "You almost had me there. If I'd have lost count, this rhubarb pie could have been really sour."

That hurled Kate into another gale of exuberant laughter. "Mama, I think you *did* lose track." She couldn't help herself, laughing uproariously, finding this original trick so hilarious. At last she caught herself. "I think you really put eighteen cups of sugar into the pie. Or was it only a half?" she teased.

Her mother laughed, love filling her soft blue eyes. "Oh Katie, sweetheart. You will never give up, will you? You caught me with that game once and the bread was too salty. After that? Hey, I've learned to be careful with you around." With that she jabbed the little girl's side, making her squeal with delight.

"Go on now. Pick up all your school things and put them away. Then come back. I've got a surprise for you."

Kate was as curious as she was fun-loving. "Surprise? What is it, Mama?" she asked, squinting past her mother, trying to see what it might be.

"No! Not now," her mother chided. "Only after you've picked up after yourself, sweets!"

Kate turned, grudgingly collecting her scattered belongings and dragging them into her bedroom where they again were quickly discarded on the floor next to her clunky, wooden desk.

Kate was already in the hallway, half-way back to the kitchen when she heard her mother calling her next instructions, "And go wash up, too. Do a good job, and use soap."

She turned around, momentarily sullen. She let out a long sigh. *Now I have to wash up. What a waste of time*, she grumbled silently.

But nothing deterred the feisty nine-year-old for long. Surely not when a surprise awaited. Faucet on; soap squirted onto grimy hands; short swish; shake-shake; hand towel. Kate didn't notice the unmistakable gray smudge she left behind on the towel before she danced back down the hallway. She never noticed dirt!

In a flash, Kate scurried to the kitchen

counter, turned her back to it and hoisted herself up onto it with muscular arms. She virtually never sat still—always running, climbing trees in the farmyard, digging up something from the black earth. Only, she didn't much like digging up potatoes or other garden produce. Worms or long discarded glass shards were so much more interesting.

"So what's the surprise, Mama? Please, tell me," she begged, pounding her fists on her strong thighs.

Her mother's eyes sparkled. She reached behind the food processor and pulled out a very large glass of ice-cold milk, and then a small plate with five molasses cookies on it.

Kate's eyes grew wide as if she were seeing a prehistoric animal. "Five?" she exclaimed with incredulity.

"Yes, five," Mama replied, reveling in the little one's joy.

Many years later, Kate's mother would share her continual fascination with the little girl's unmatched sense of wonder—the most simple things would elicit a response as animated as if she had been presented with a priceless gem. And then, a grown Kate would reply, "But Mama, who except you could put up with me and see the good in my antics?"

"Thank you, thank you, thank you, Mama!" Kate swooned, head tilted back, eyes closed as if she had been in profound anticipation of this treat of a lifetime.

In reality, this treat was regularly part of the Woodson household because every one of the four girls loved molasses cookies. They were Daddy's favorites, too. But somehow, Mama had a way of playing each of the four girls' games. Kate's were the mischievous, playful ones—and anything involving sweets.

To be sure, Kate was hardly ever awarded *five* cookies at one time, so she was wasn't feigning her astonishment over that. As she bit into the first one, reaching to take a big gulp of milk, she began to tell stories. Story after story poured from her little heart as she sat on the kitchen counter. Her mother heard tales of who cheated in the social studies quiz, who hit a home run in the recess softball game, and who had a brand new pair of purple and black socks. Some days there were tears over nasty comments her best friend made; another day frustration about missing one hundred percent on a spelling test because she spelled the word "cartoon" as "carton." She knew how to spell *cartoon*, she lamented in tears. Why wouldn't the teacher give her a second chance?

"Mama, how many teaspoons of salt did you put in these cookies?" Kate asked, mouth stuffed with her fourth cookie.

Mama just laughed. This little one was unstoppable.

"I bet you don't know, Mama," she exclaimed.

Mama came to stand right in front of Kate, holding the child's head between her two hands. "I know for *sure* how many, sweets." she said with great seriousness. Then more laughter. "But, look at your mouth! Go wash up, and then you can practice piano."

Kate made a face, but jumped down.

"Ninety-nine!" she called back. "That's how many teaspoons!"

Uncontainable laughter.

Hoods

　　It was an uncomfortable day in early June—the second day of summer vacation after Kenya's first year of *middle school*. Whatever *that* was. She lay sprawled on the living room floor, in direct line of a weak fan, vacantly paging through a book she'd been *encouraged* to read. She loved to read. That wasn't the problem. But *she* would have loved to decide what she would read during her free time.

　　The sharp pounding on the front door, mere inches from where she lay, jerked her body to attention. Terror instantly invaded her dark eyes. The last time this had happened in their economically depressed neighborhood, *their* house had been targeted by a loud, demanding group of hooded men. Who were they? What did they want? Why were they dressed like that? Her mother had been vague and had tried to brush it off, but her blue eyes had revealed her own panic.

　　Her heart pounded as her stepfather strode to the door. "Kenya, get outta here. *Now*!" he barked as he passed. Quick as a hummingbird, she flitted under the table in the adjacent room.

　　Her stepfather was a minister in a small rural church made up exclusively of *white folk*. Except for her, of course. She was "black". At least that's what *he* had told her years ago. She never referred to her stepfather by his given name and she refused to call him Dad. Her *real* dad was a pharmacist in the city. She saw him on holidays.

She could hear his voice, low and tersely appeasing. "No, brothers," he spat out, "I am *with* you. I am one of you! Don't forget that!"

Kenya slowly peered around the corner, then pulled a breath in sharply. Hoods! She disappeared and slunk to the far end under the table. More loud, almost indistinguishable sounds from under formidable hoods. She could only make out a few words. "... *she* has to go ..." and "... *she's* not one of us ...."

Instinctively she knew whom they were talking about. A cold shiver ran down her sweaty back. Horror gripped her. She had once wanted to check out a book from the library that had a picture of people dressed in white hoods on the jacket, but her mother had quickly snatched if from her, stating it was "unsuitable." And because she didn't go to school, she had never had the opportunity to ask anyone about it.

The voices hissed and droned, rose and fell. They were not giving in and neither was her stepfather. She could tell by his voice that he was getting angry.

But why? Why her? "Not one of us?" Why not? Her family lived here; they went to church here; she went to the store with her mother and four half-brothers and sisters here.

"You're black. You're black. You're black." The words she'd heard from *him* years ago reverberated through her brain.

"No, I'm not!" she had argued, looking down at her pale cappuccino colored arm. She had been four. "I'm not black! I'm ... I'm beige," she had insisted, having just learned various nuances of color.

But there had been no arguing. She was black. *He* had said so.

Kenya's entire body shook with humiliation and fear. She didn't like who she was. When she was old enough to run away, she would go to the hair salon and have them put light brown dye into her hair. Like her granny's hair. Her hair was soft and always smelled good.

But, of course, she hadn't seen her granny in a very long time because she had been there when *he* had called her black. Granny had said *black* was lovely, but that she could be *beige* if she wished. Granny had fought for her. For her "Baby Kenya" as she'd called her. No one called her *Baby Kenya* now and she longed to hear that voice again. Not that she was a baby, but because her granny said she would always love her no matter what.

He stormed back into the house, slamming the door. Rage was in his step. Her thoughts went quickly to what might come next.

"Ken? Where are you?" She hated being called *Ken*. That was a boy's name, but he hated *Kenya,* as he said it made her sound like she belonged in *Africa.* And that must always remind him that she wasn't white. Not the *perfect, holy, Sunday-school-picture* color that he said he and her mother and siblings were.

His shoes appeared next to the table near her and he stooped to peer underneath. "Get outta there," he snarled, grabbing her right arm even though she was already wiggling her body out.

"Stop that! That hurts," she wailed, not even looking into his steely eyes. "Robot eyes" is what she called them. But only to herself. Never out loud.

He shook her again. "*You!* You're to blame for all of this! If you weren't ... *black."* He heaved her arm down with disgust and turned to leave the room. "If that damn girl weren't...," he spat at Kenya's mother, "...a...a fuckin'...," he paused again. Furious.

Kenya knew all too well which word he *meant* to use. He'd used it so often in the past and it had broken her. "If we didn't have *her*," his words were laced with contempt, "We wouldn't have these problems."

Her head dropped; tears collected in her eyes; fists clenched. Every time he lashed out, he left her destroyed. Humiliated. Violated. Discarded.

Something moved in the doorway and she knew it was her mother without even lifting her face. When she finally turned, she saw her weary mother mouth the words, "I'm sorry."

Quickly Kenya went to her room and threw herself onto the bed, sobs wrenching her body. She wished more than anything that she could go far away, color her hair and read any book she wanted.

One day I will, she vowed. *You wait—one day I will.*

Removing Labels

"A coveted label on a pair of sneakers can increase their value by fifty percent or more. Brand name labels are equated with quality, prestige and desirability. Removing or damaging the label renders the product virtually worthless."

Hmm. That's a revealing statement on the state of this culture, muses Therese—a journalist by profession, amateur researcher and detective by hobby. Since she isn't particularly known for wearing designer clothing, she opts not to read the entire article.

Another story in the local paper captures her attention: *"Houston woman found dead in shallow lake outside Austin city limits."* That's close to home.

The article tells a gruesome story of "torture with a sharp object, blunt force trauma, rape and the use of bleach, presumably to destroy evidence." The woman is described as "a homeless, drug-addicted prostitute, with a record of numerous prior arrests."

Reason for murder: "theft totaling less than two hundred dollars in merchandise."

Two hundred dollars? Therese looks up from her tablet briefly, takes another sip from her steaming Chai latte. Why? Why would someone kill over a class B misdemeanor? Such a travesty.

Therese reads on to discover that, according to neighborhood witnesses, the victim, Sydney Kathleen Collins, had been seen in the company of the murder suspects on numerous occasions. All three suspects had multiple previous convictions ranging from domestic assault and battery, to drug possession and distribution, to armed theft. Apparently a noisy confrontation had broken out just after noon on July 4 in a third floor apartment, which is said to have been used for business purposes by the three suspects. Ms. Collins, allegedly appearing confused, had been seen entering the apartment earlier.

Therese continues to read whatever the Internet will divulge regarding Sydney Kathleen Collins. She hates the labels people put on others— labels that somehow make senseless crimes seem less horrific. Removed. Distant. It's unconscionable to victimize Sydney further through labels, she fumes: a whore, crackhead, drifter and thief. Who was this woman?

Therese was scheduled for vacation the following three weeks, and after she returned to the office, her workload seemed to double. A short time later came Thanksgiving, Christmas and New Years, making it more than six months before she felt she could again allow herself the luxury of researching stories that were not directly work related.

By this time, articles giving more depth to the murdered woman's life were readily available. Apparently some journalists still place value on a human element, Therese observed.

But what proved to be Therese's jackpot was Sydney's mother's blog. Since her daughter's death, the older woman, retired from social work, had begun paying tribute to Sydney's life. Here, in moving prose and poetry, she chronicled her daughter's early years, struggles, joys, her slide into drug addiction and abuse, and culminating with her violent death. It was powerfully poignant.

In addition to Sydney's mother's tributes, friends offered their memories: "Sydney was a deep thinker; always helpful," wrote one. Another added, "She did love to party. I recall when she met and fell in love with Carl. That seems to be when the slide began." *The slide* apparently alluding to Sydney's struggle with illegal substances.

Sydney's colleagues from a law firm described her as "very smart, a gifted poet who loved the beach." They too lamented the rapid decline into addiction.

Therese allowed this tragedy to settle over her for a moment. She thought about her older sister who was around the same age Sydney had been when she was murdered. What if it had been her? What would that feel like?

As she brushed through her wet hair the following morning, she saw an email from a highly respected, local domestic violence advocate in her unread mail. Therese and Melanie had been friends ever since they had both worked on a volatile family law case. This time, Melanie wrote to select members of her mailing list, asking for volunteers to sit in on the trial of Sydney Kathleen Collins' alleged killers. Ms. Collins had been an only child, Melanie explained, and therefore, her mother would be the only family member present in the courtroom. Melanie felt that community support should be strong, and that the memory of this victim of violence be honored. The trial was slated to begin in a month, and was expected to last the better part of a week.

"Mr. Blackwood, could I have the first week of March off?" Therese asked as soon as she arrived at the office.

Her supervisor countered with no clarifying questions, even though Therese had enjoyed an extended vacation within the past half year. She was an excellent journalist and gave the publication desk one hundred fifty percent when she was at work.

"Absolutely, Terry," he agreed, one of the few people who got by with abbreviating her name.

"Thanks! I appreciate it, sir," she smiled.

Therese wore black all week. It only seemed right.

She took a tiny linen-covered notebook and pen into the courtroom with her. Even though she wasn't there in an official capacity, she wanted to capture some impressions of who Sydney Kathleen Collins had been.

Prosecutors' evidence was gripping. Defense attorneys countered with attempts to discredit testimony. The visual testimony created a picture of sordid and appalling proportions. Defendants sat uncomfortably in crisp suits, slouched, listening, sometimes sneering. Therese observed each one.

She sat through it hour after hour, day after day, uttering not one word. She was not there as a reporter or a trial witness. She was there to *bear witness*. To honor. To mourn the loss of a person—a woman of worth, potential and value.

Hearing a guilty verdict seemed only a partial victory. Justice had been served; now labels must systematically, humanely and accurately be removed. Only in removing labels could dignity be restored; value returned.

She wore white for the event. Smiling, she signed each copy of the book with,

In honor of Sydney,
No more labels.
–Therese Grant

She Spoke My Name

>~

The coffee shop was loud. Crowded. Hissing espresso machines, ice clanking in tall glasses, customers laughing—all sounds that CJ adored about this place. It had been years since she'd been here–in her old hometown. Yes, she had been born here, but her real experience with this coastal tourist town had been limited to her first five years of life. And a few return trips on weekends during college.

It was here—*Café Noir*—that she had practically cut her first teeth. Her mother (whom she affectionately called "Mam") and grandmother (Noni) had schlepped her here from as early on as she could remember. They met after work, before Saturday market, for Sunday brunch. Anytime either of them grew weary of life's daily grayness.

She looked around with pleasure. The place had grown, she observed wistfully. That must mean business was good. A smile snuck across her face as she set her bag down and nestled into a chair at a corner table. She pulled out a lightweight cardigan, remembering how southern coastal restaurants were so inordinately over air-conditioned during the summer months.

CJ hoped to find solace in this town for the next two, possibly three days. She had a publishing deadline by the end of the week, and her home turf was not proving conducive to writing right now. Here she could relax—her identity concealed, as she was nearly a household name now in her current neighborhood, and definitely among abnormal psychology novel enthusiasts around the globe.

Peering at the screen of her sleek tablet, her mind meandered back to another day, in this town, when her mother's brand-new boyfriend, James, had announced that she, Camille Jeanna Pelletier would no longer be known as Camille, or Millie—as Mam used to teasingly call her. James resented her French-born father, who, he claimed, was nothing more than an uppity deadbeat dad. Mam had argued that point vigorously at the beginning of this romance, but James' jealousy would tolerate no challenge. So, while her surname would still reflect her paternal side, her initials, "CJ," would replace her lyrical given names, Camille Jeanna.

She remembered how horrified she had been at this prospect as a small child. How could someone—anyone—steal her name? It wasn't right! She was *Camille*, and that was that! In her childish innocence she, too, had fought the newly imposed regime. Hands on hips she had declared bravely, "But I don't *want* to have the name CJ. That's boring and ..."

James had interrupted sharply, "Girl, I don't care what *you* want. I'm not going to remember that bastard every time I hear your name."

Camille—CJ—had been deeply humiliated and frightened, having had no idea what his words meant. She had begun to sob out of the sheer horror of being ignored. And insulted. Mam had always listened to what she wanted, even when she couldn't actually have what she desired. And Mam didn't scream. Or interrupt.

Even now CJ could feel the terror—how she had felt stripped bare. Separated from ... from what? She hadn't known then. But now CJ was quite aware of the onion-like layers of alienation she had been subjected to. It had begun with herself. That day. She had been denied the right to continue being herself. And that had only been the beginning, she recalled, a spreading shadow darkening her young face.

All of the turmoil and torment she had experienced over the years had inspired her to study psychology. So she went to the Université Paris Descartes—a bit of French spite, she acknowledged bitterly. She had been only nineteen. She had studied feverishly and had mastered French. It was here that she had begun to write stories. Many stories. A great multitude of stories. Most of them had been her own personal stories, long trapped within, now pouring forth like water, gushing from an overflowing drainage pipe after a spring thaw.

CJ stared into the comforting space of her childhood haven. Once she had left here, her life had been nothing short of tumultuous. No, that term wasn't nearly strong enough. What she had lived through had been abuse. Unequivocal, subversive abuse. Now she could see it.

She caught herself, shook her head almost imperceptibly as if to hit a restart button. Her eyes focused on her manuscript once more. She reread the previous ten pages, again dipping down into the sordid story. This novel depicted the nuances of a psychotic, manipulating personality, the mastery of mind-controlling techniques used to deceive countless people.

She was a masterful storyteller and an authority on the subject—both experientially and clinically. She wrote furiously, taking an occasional sip from her *bol de café*. She loved this "latte in a breakfast bowl" because it reminded her of her years in France. The scene she now wrote relayed a particularly heartwarming conversation between mother and estranged daughter. The two had again found each other after many years of isolation. Tentative at first, daring to question and share, trusting a little more each time. So much was biographical; yet it partially reflected deep-seated longings.

Her eyes lifted, staring into the opposite corner of the café. How could it be that *one person* could wield enough power to control entire families? Groups? Communities? But it was real: she had lived it, and studied it.

"Camille?" Startled, CJ glanced in the direction of her name. She recognized no one.

"Camille, darling?" A tall, square-shouldered woman with snow-white hair approached her apprehensively.

CJ's heart nearly stopped. *N*o. It couldn't be. She had wondered if Noni still lived here. For years she had been told Noni disdained her.

"Noni?" CJ rose quickly from her chair. The women fell into a long, sobbing embrace.

"Oh darling, Camille," the older woman whispered over and over.

Her name. Her *own* name! It smoothed the wrinkles from her parched soul.

That Small Child

There she lies, disheveled golden hair on her smooth cotton pillow case. She stretches out on her king-sized bed, then quickly turns on her side, drawing her legs up tightly to her chest. Her body is tense; her mind in turmoil. A small light gleams its warmth from the outlet next to the armoire. Outside, the wind howls.

"What was *that*?" she asks herself, wide-eyed, replaying the tumultuous interchange between her and the team of "experts" commissioned to extricate the internal demons supposedly haunting her. When she had been admonished, then prodded, and finally forced to denounce "that small child she once was," she had resisted, sensing intuitively, that something was terribly wrong.

She was stunned. The experts had sided with *him*—declaring *she* was responsible for evil's ravages within her. She continued to mentally rehearse all that had taken place mere hours ago. Only through enormous effort had she been able to summon her voice to utter a clear, unmistakable, *"no"*. Then a second and third *"no, no, never."* Trembling in fear, she did everything within her power to regain control of her own thoughts. Only through tremendous mental exertion had she been able to rise.

And then another battle had ensued: she against the experts.

They: "You *must* go through with this; your very soul is in peril."

She: "I can't continue. *She* is who *I am*."

Now here she lies, body rigid with anxiety, guilt and torment. Renewed trauma. Dreading a psychotic break. She fears sleep, yet is haunted in wakefulness. After four-and-a-half motionless hours she drifts into an unforgiving sleep.

Tossing back and forth. Guttural moans. Arms reaching; finding nothing. Muffled, indistinguishable words. Vacant, wide eyes.

> ~~~

In another time, in a remote house, threadbare curtains allowed the faint flicker of a distant streetlight, struggling through the sleet, to create grotesque shadows on the dingy wall.

The room was sparsely furnished—a grinning teddy bear slouched atop a child-sized chair with bold blue paint peeling to expose bare wood; a miniature chest, one drawer open, the other closed; a small wooden box sheltering aging toys; a narrow, wire-framed child's bed with pillow and faded quilt. That was all.

The wisp of a child, legs drawn up close to her chest, lay motionless on the sagging mattress. Her tiny body shivered as she drew the flimsy quilt over her thin shoulders.

From the edges of the musty curtains, what appeared to her as a single tendril of ethereal smoke curled around and up to the corner of the ceiling. Then another slunk out from a crack in the floor slat; still another from each electrical outlet. Without stirring, the small child's terrified eyes darted back and forth. Her muscles tightened imperceptibly. Her breath came in short spurts.

Then his enraged voice filled her troubled mind, evoking terror within her fragile soul.

"Say you're sorry!"

"You're to blame."

"It's all your fault."

"Your lying has to stop."

"Come here. I need to whip this outta you."

She flinched involuntarily, forcing her eyes to close over the welling tears. Darkness was no refuge. She hated the dark, but he would allow no light at night. She didn't understand. Even a small light that would disturb no one would help. Help to keep the smoke from snaking over the walls, the floor, her bed. Help to keep the voice from raging in her head. Help to give her a sense that all was not cold. Unforgiving. Demanding. Painful. Oh yes, so very painful.

"Satan's got a hold of you, girl."

How she ached for peace.

"You shouldn't have let him."

Thundering. Accusing. Violating. She could not stop his voice from shouting in her mind. And she was so debilitatingly cold.

If only she could call her mother. Mother had always comforted her. Held her. Stroked her long golden hair. But he would not allow that now. He said she needed to be good. And then he would rage and scream and try to force some unseen force from her.

When he was like that she was immobilized and terrified. So she did her best to listen. To obey. To cooperate. Not to get angry or to lie. If he so much as suspected she was lying, he would beat her to an inch of her life. Except she couldn't express that until decades later.

Oh, the dread. The panic. She feared whatever he labeled "Satan". It must be horrible. Like a hundred darknesses and a thousand beatings. But it was his tormenting of her—not whatever Satan was—that froze her muscles and paralyzed her tongue. She could neither move nor speak. Only her eyes conveyed the horror. But no one could see her eyes that night. Or how she lay on her lumpy mattress. Desperately seeking warmth from her frayed quilt.

She saw her balding teddy bear on the chair, but dared not retrieve him. If she did, she would become visible to whatever it was that swirled in the night. She chided herself for not thinking to bring her beloved companion with her earlier.

"You!"

There it was again. His voice—not really *his* voice, but how she remembered his screaming voice when they were all still awake. She, her mother, her older sister. And *he*.

"You! Come here."
"Why didn't you ...?"
"Didn't I tell you ...?"
"How's it you never learn a thing?"

She buried her face in the quilt, stifling the sobs that wracked her tiny body. She didn't know what he meant or what she had done. He said it was all because she had let Satan ... let Satan do something. She didn't know what. She didn't even understand what Satan was.

⌐⌐

Perspiration-soaked, gasping for air, she bolts upright from her cotton pillowcase. Certain her chest will burst and her eyes fly out of their sockets, she forces herself to inhale and exhale. Over and over. A quarter hour. Breathing. Clutching her blanket. Calming that small child within her.

Sapphire Trae McKesson

～

Already at eight, Sapphire had fought her way to being included in the boys' football team at her decrepit grade school, right in the middle of what some termed "urban squalor." She could keep up with the worst—and the best. Vulgarities spewed from her mouth without venom, reflecting the commonality of such language in every part of her environment. Her boisterous laughter revealed gaping holes where permanent teeth ought to have been, but instead had been cruelly beaten from her tiny face by one of her mother's capricious boyfriends. Her oddly unmatched clothing was often held together with oversized safety pins or belts, which could be swiftly called upon to double as weapons when threatened–which happened regularly. More than once a much bigger boy had howled in pain, finding his hindquarters the target of the sharp tip of a rusty pin.

"Aggressives"—the derogatory term coined by stern administrators for the segment of the student population who they felt caused concern—seemed to fit perfectly. Yet, unlike many other aggressives, Sapphire rarely instigated trouble, but could hold her own handily when provoked, or when she saw a defenseless person or animal being treated unfairly. She was also known to attack her studies in the same way she did her adversaries: with tenacity, fearlessness and passion. Those she fought on the playground or streets shook their heads in confusion at her dizzying intelligence–easily and willingly expressed.

It was a humid August afternoon, when the crumbling concrete radiates oven-hot, foul air–a noiseless reminder of dead rats, cheap grilled steaks, feces, urine and blood-stained sidewalks, choking mixtures of illegal substances and vehicle exhaust. No one much noticed or cared. Sapphire exploded out of the kitchen door of her row house, followed by an entourage of five equally rambunctious children. She kicked a rock in front of her as she strode ahead, hands in her pockets, looking for something to do.

Across from the twisted basketball hoop fastened to the neighboring housing unit, a group of older boys shouted and danced, always returning to squat down at one spot on the ground next to the fence. Her eyes narrowed, curious, but all the while silently assessing the advisability of going any nearer. She knew all but one of the boys. They were nine or ten years old and much bigger than she. Yet she wondered what the commotion was about.

A tiny yelp pierced the blazing afternoon, and Sapphire bounded into a sprint, looking over her shoulder just long enough to shout a commanding, "C'mon!" Not waiting for anyone to follow, she was next to the rowdy boys in under a minute.

She didn't even have to ask, "Wassup?" Immediately she saw the cowering, shaking ball of matted fur the boys were tormenting. Egging each other on, the boys kicked, teased and harassed what appeared to be a tiny dog that had no way to escape. She had no idea what kind of dog it was, but no one– not any person, regardless of size–would mistreat a dog in her presence. Her blood boiled and her fists clenched.

"Stop that, you fucking assholes," Sapphire spat at the boys. The biggest of the boys, two grades ahead of her and known to already be part of a neighborhood gang, looked at her with derision. He turned to face her, legs apart, arms crossed over his chest.

"Yo! Whaddaya want?" No answer. Sapphire was on a mission. He tried again, "Hey, bitch. You'd better watch it."

She paid his pretentious posturing no mind, strode into the middle of the boys towards the terrified animal, frozen in a heap, awaiting the next, inevitable blow.

The boys were ready to tackle her, but the ringleader gave them a silent sign to stand down. She sat, right beside the whimpering dog next to the fence, six boys now forming a tight circle around her so that neither of them could escape. She tried to remain calm, undaunted, though noticing her vulnerable position, her heart began beating furiously.

Don't think about that now, she scolded herself. Sapphire began to stroke the tiny creature's head without moving or lifting him in any way, having no idea what kind of injury he had suffered. She had learned that from reading veterinary medicine books. Quietly she began talking to him— soothing, comforting. The boys stayed in position, muscles flexing, impatient with their leader, determined not to let this brat get the better of them. They had every right to take care of the filthy vermin that infested their neighborhood.

After several agonizing moments, the

wounded pup–certainly no more than a few months old–slowly hobbled nearer to Sapphire, then onto her lap. Two of the boys made motions that they needed to end this, but the ringleader stopped them with a scowl.

Sapphire's head began to swirl. How would she get herself and the wounded animal to safety? She was sitting, and therefore in no position to put up a fight. But she would never leave this mistreated animal alone. Never. These boys could kick them both unconscious, but it would be together.

Before thinking about the next move, she shouted to her friends standing some distance from the threatening circle, "Bri, get my momma!"

No one could ever have predicted what followed. Sapphire's mother was actually home, and sober. The boys began to hesitate, and one by one they disbursed. At the animal clinic, a few minutes later, she described what had happened.

"Yes, doctor."

"No, doctor."

"Thank you, doctor."

He was a terrier mix. She called him Taurean, meaning "strength."

"We'll call you when you can pick him up," they promised.

Sapphire left in silence. In the coming days she was unusually somber. She visited Taurean daily and threw herself into her studies.

Weeks later, the principal called her name in

the school assembly. "Sapphire Trae McKesson–honored for the heroic rescue of an abused animal."

The first of many awards.

Under Cover of Darkness

It was a sultry September evening—unusually suffocating for this time of year. Swarms of insects droned and fought their way toward the light at the window screen, but she hardly noticed as she shuffled toward the shabby bed, set in the middle of the narrow room. Instinctively she reached forward to extinguish the light from the single bulb that served as a false beacon to the buzzing, fluttering winged army a few feet away.

She sat down heavily on the side of the bed, not because she was a big woman, nor because she would necessarily be classified as old. She was weary. Preoccupied. Laden with a myriad of experiences, tepid hopes, dashed dreams, recurring disappointments, insatiable longings, shadowy fears. One hand pushed the unruly dark curls away from her face, her eyes closing as her head fell backwards. Of what use was it? She had tried every conceivable angle to reconcile, restore, resurrect and redirect. Nothing. She had tried as best she could to reason with the parents—her very own children—to allow her further contact with her firstborn grandson. They had been inseparable since his birth.

But absolutely nothing had changed the fact that this child—this innocent, panic-stricken, pining and begging child—was no longer allowed to even see her face or hear his beloved Nana's voice.

Nana. Only Cooper had ever called her that. They had been one heart and one soul. But that was nearly four years ago. Now there had been four years of silence. No contact. She wasn't even sure where her daughter and new son-in-law had moved since they had left town abruptly without a word. Mutual acquaintances had informed her of the birth of Cooper's baby sister a year ago. A year ago today. Unthinkable, that on this day in September one year ago, a new sweet child had been born into her family, but she knew not where, had never been personally informed and knew no name.

Her weary form slumped sideways, her head falling onto the pillow. She lay there staring without seeing. Wondering. Crying with no tears. Mind a-whir without words. Formless, shapeless agonies gnawing at her soul.

The hours wore on. One o'clock. Half past. Two o'clock. Her form stirred slightly, then resumed complete stillness. A breeze caressed the billowing flimsy purple curtains, and through the screened opening, a fog filled the room. The muted purple haze melded with the amorphous gloom, carrying an unsettling quality with it.

His outline was vague, but there was no mistaking the shock of blond framing the childish face. He stood motionless, allowing the swirling traces of indistinct color to first obscure then reveal his position near the corner of the room.

She moved almost imperceptibly.

"Nana?" a nearly inaudible whisper fluttered from the shrouded corner. A moment passed. "Nana, wake up."

Again, a leg moved, as if registering a slight cramp.

"Nana." This time the voice revealed a more agitated tone. "I need to talk with you."

Instantly she sat upright, swinging her legs over the edge of the bed. She rubbed her eyes, peering into the darkness. It was a heavily clouded night, so the moon offered no assistance for her vision.

"Nana," the voice spoke, increasing in intensity.

She rose quickly to faltering limbs, bending down to stabilize her sleepy body. She reached into the haze from where the voice had come, groping aimlessly until she touched something. Someone.

"Cooper?" she questioned, doubting her own perception, justifying her query simply because he–someone–had addressed her as Nana. His arms found her and wrapped themselves around her. "Oh Cooper," she wept out loud. "Cooper."

"Nana, I miss you so much. Where have you been?" The words tumbled almost incomprehensibly from his fragile frame.

She took hold of his shoulders, moving his body slightly away from hers so she could see his upturned face. His eyes questioning and pained. Involuntarily a sob choked her chest, tears clouding her eyes.

"Cooper, oh Cooper!" was all her mouth, which seemed as if it contained cotton, would produce. She felt dumb. Unable to formulate words. Paralyzed and lame. "Cooper, dear child." They embraced once more and stayed this way. For how long she didn't know. Seconds? Minutes? She thought she must find something of meaning to say. Something comforting. Something loving. Something valuable, as who knew when they would see one another again. No words came and she chided herself inwardly for her frozen immobility.

Her body twitched. Her eyes instantly opened. Her breath rapid. A chill ran down her bare arms. She lay facing the open window, now noiseless and vacant. The sheer curtains moved slightly against the screen. The tension in her body gave way to anguished convulsing, as she heaved under the weight of alienation. Tears flowed from her wrinkled eyes, seeping down into the pillow beneath her head. As countless other tears had done on countless other nights.

Daddy, I Got This!

⤜

July 18 promised to be a day like all other hot, gloriously unpredictable summer farm days. Sarah had already done her morning chores and had settled in to draw at the kitchen table. At age ten, when she wasn't absorbed in one aspect of outside adventure or another, she drew faces on endless scraps of paper. All kinds of faces: sullen, grinning, scowling, staring. And since no one in her family ventured into amateur personality analysis, no one wondered about this quirky obsession.

"Quit wasting your time with all those caricatures," her practical mother joked. "Go practice piano instead."

But Sarah had no interest in piano during the summer vacation. In fact, nothing was further from her mind. Summer was her time to draw—or to bound unfettered over acres of farmland, hair flying, nothing on her feet but calluses as thick as the rind on the enormous slabs of pork beside her breakfast pancakes.

This morning seemed no different. She had already fed the chickens, milked the cows, and—already at age ten—she had seen to it that the ancient VW Beetle could sputter awake and be coaxed to lurch round the farmyard.

It was only a matter of time until the soaring outdoor temperatures would again lure her away from her more focused, artistic ventures to explore without supervision or boundary. But for now she sat in rare stillness—pencil in hand, pursuing another pastime.

She heard a noisy vehicle pull up next to the farmhouse, but paid no mind. Already her mother was at the screen door, calling a welcome to whoever it was. Sarah couldn't hear what the visitor said, but her mother's response peaked her interest.

"No, he's not home right now. Is there something you need?"

A torrent of high-pitched words. She'd know that voice anywhere, having heard it often enough. It was Mr. Braxton, the farmer who lived with his wife and nine young children almost three miles straight east of them.

"Well, I don't know, Mr. Braxton. I have no idea..." her voice trailed. Then rallying quickly, she offered, "But, I think Sarah might know."

Now Sarah was curious. What might "Sarah know," she wondered, her neck stretching, rising halfway from her chair to peer over the window sill and out to the yard.

"Sarah, Mr. Braxton wants to use the tractor, but doesn't know how to start it," her mother declared matter-of-factly, walking through the door.

The small girl's eyes gleamed as she shrugged her shoulders. Not many people knew how to fire up the old John Deere diesels that needed starting with a pony motor and many complicated steps. But, she'd watched her daddy do it countless times.

"Sarah," said her mother again, interrupting her thoughts, "Can you come out here and show Mr. Braxton how to start it?"

Without a second thought Sarah jumped out of her chair and bounded through the screen door, letting it slam behind her. Good thing she'd actually put on more than underwear and a t-shirt that morning, she thought. Often she didn't.

Walking out to the machine shed with Sarah, Mr. Braxton looked a little sheepish, and his voice grated on and on about needing the tractor and how her daddy had told him he could use it. He lamented that he had no idea how to start "the beast."

Sarah bristled slightly, quite protective of her daddy's machinery, equipment, animals and land. At the time she didn't know that she would qualify as a regular tomboy—learning the term only much later on. All that mattered today was leading Mr. Braxton to the shed, climbing up onto the massive green tractor and turning switches, pulling levers and pushing buttons till the first motor—then the second—sprang to life. Sarah had always loved the rhythmic *put-put* of the shiny John Deere tractor. Now she sat tall and proud, almost as if she and Deerey—her pet name for the machine—had a secret agreement to lavish delight on one another.

But her task was completed. Mr. Braxton needed to move on. So, she carefully picked her way down from the heights. Her sinewy, tanned legs stepped on first one firm landing spot then to another until she again stood squarely on the ground. She watched as Mr. Braxton made his way out of the shed and into the yard. Soon the *put-put* of the motor faded as Deerey disappeared down the road.

Sarah could focus on little else that day, waiting for her daddy's return. As soon as the stylish lemon-yellow Pontiac came to a stop in front of the house, she danced out with childish effervescence. Her daddy scooped her up, still able to pick her up easily, though she was almost eleven. There were the routine tickles, shrieks and giggles until she fought to free herself, bouncing to the ground.

"Know what, Daddy?" she asked animatedly.

The bronzed, short man grabbed her hand, "No, jumping bean, I don't. You tell me!"

A smile as bright as the noonday sun enveloped her entire being. Jumping bean—only one of the many names Daddy had invented for his fourth and final daughter. His dark eyes reflected her joy.

"I helped Mr. Braxton today."

"You did? How did you do that?"

"He came to get Deerey," she explained.

"Okay, then what?"

"Uh ... well, he didn't know how to start her, so I helped."

Daddy stopped in his tracks as if he were too surprised to carry on. His hands flew up and apart, "You did *what?*" he asked with contrived astonishment.

This game always made Sarah dissolve into such a fit of belly laughter that she doubled over, holding her sides.

"Oh, Daddy!" she yelled. "You know I've seen you do it ... I've watched you a hundred times."

That was true. She was always at his side and Daddy knew it. His eyes gleamed.

Whose Truth?

〜

Why does she wrestle with guilt and doubt daily? Is she who she says she is? Is she real? Authentic? Can she trust her own opinions and intuition, or would she do well to have someone else make decisions for her? Even small decisions send her into a heart-pounding tailspin—like what outfit to wear to the company party or what kind of take-out she wants on a Friday evening. She has no idea why. This debilitating self-scrutiny encroaches on her soaring career and strains the few relationships she has managed to retain.

With every passing day she becomes more unsure and therefore, more concerned about how to carry on. Maybe she should see a therapist. Maybe her priest. Maybe she truly is going crazy.

Or maybe she is going to hell.

At that thought, her entire body tenses and sweat pours from her forehead. *Hell*. For years she has pushed that concept as far away as possible, yet it resurfaces at the most inopportune times.

Everything about her personal beliefs has changed over the past two decades. Well, nearly everything. She does believe in God and finds comfort in her spirituality. But hell? She shudders in recollection of her childhood.

She can never completely reign in her thoughts when they *go there* and today seems worse than ever. She pulls her thunder gray Mini Cooper into the double garage attached to her exclusive country home. She stumbles into the house, throws her coat and briefcase onto the couch in her den and collapses into the soft suede easy chair.

Everything she owns is *real*. Everything. Leather; hardwood; crystal; silver; suede. She wears only wool, raw silk, cotton or linen. She cannot tolerate imitation. She's fanatical about authenticity.

Her hand moves back and forth over the armrest. It's *real*. Representing a truth of sorts.

Tell the truth, girl. Her shoulders jerk involuntarily. She would recognize that voice on Tiananmen Square at noon. Shame, doubt and fear wash over her in waves.

The five-year-old child had spoken her truth to a preschool teacher that fateful day in December. The memory had never left her, but had been buried under layers of blame, shame, arguments, accusations, continual attempts to please, prayers for healing, sermons about truth and a pathological obsession for perfection.

Old theatrical characters re-emerge out of the dingy backstage of her mind. A flurry of uniformed people, doctors, nurses, teachers, counselors—in schools, hospitals, professional offices and at home. But the most terrifying of all are her mom and dad. Each of them had held one of her shoulders, demanding that she tell the *real* truth. Not some fairytale they believed she was making up. Just remember: *There was absolutely no way he could have done that to her.*

She had been tormented. She thought she had told the truth when she spoke with the teacher. She hadn't a reason not to. Her teacher had said, "You can always tell me anything." That's what she had done. She was terribly confused. She cried. She was beaten. She was grilled relentlessly. She was told so frequently that her story was wrong that she began to believe an alternate story. It wasn't her truth. It was what they demanded truth to be.

Her spoken truth had plummeted her into never-ending anguish, terror, discrimination from those in her own home, and existential doubt about her spirituality. Only, as a child, she had had no idea that this was happening.

Tonight, overcome with reemerging recollections, her body slowly crumples into an unrecognizable heap in her perfect suede chair. Oh, the countless whippings for "not telling the truth." The hundreds of hands groping her body as men and women tried to "pray her right." The perpetual stares of other children and their parents. Then, chilling threats. Now, once again, she almost became that forlorn child she thought she had left behind.

How this one truth-telling episode had spiraled her down into the dungeon of shame, self-hatred and insecurity. The paralyzing inferiority—an entrenched part of her persona—was so much more tolerable than the fear that she could not decipher truth. She could no longer trust herself to know her own truth. She had failed to discern once, at age five, and others' truth had been pounded into her mind, soul and body from that day forward.

This unbearable reality had thrust her out of her own home when she was barely eighteen. She had reeled, staggered, nearly drowned in confusion and rejection. She had no longer been welcome.

She had sat for hours, days, possibly weeks in the same position she found herself in tonight. She should just end it all, she reasoned now—just as she had back then. Who would care? They would probably rejoice! But she was incapable of even managing that feat, she observed with disgust. Too unsure. *How would I choose to die? What would be least painful? Where would I get what I needed to do it? What if my body isn't discovered for weeks?*

She can still see the terrified teenager on a threadbare couch, floating between dehydrated delirium and agitated sleep. In her stupor she had heard a knock at the door. She had been dreadfully startled, fearing the caller would see to it that she was committed to a mental institution.

She had not answered the door that night. But she had answered. She had responded to the desire to live. She had determined she could face this irreparably bleak world on her own. She would rise. She had to.

She had summoned the courage to make decisions for the first time in her life: she found work, applied for scholarships, went to school and graduated with distinction. She still held the prestigious position she'd been offered immediately after graduation.

Many considered her a rising star, the recipient of admiring glances. But whose "truth" was that really? That, too, may be a delusion of her twisted soul.

By Your Words

A dull-gray scarf hangs over her skeletal shoulders like dense fog shrouding jagged coastal rocks. She stops just inside, vacant eyes searching every corner of the nearly filled classroom. She clutches her fraying bag, appearing to momentarily consider a swift exit.

A tall, engaging woman at the head of the classroom directs her warm eyes to the newcomer, waving her in with a smile. "C'mon in!" she welcomes. "There's still room here at this table."

As the newcomer makes her way past other participants, she nears the empty chair. The instructor stretches out a strong, olive hand. "Amanda Walker," she offers, shaking her hand. "But, just call me Mandy."

The newcomer lifts her head, offering a hand in return. "Carmen," she whispers, "...*just Carmen.*"

"Welcome, Carmen," says Mandy. Carmen smiles vaguely. Absently. So this must be the woman who will lead this creative writing class she had signed up for. Carmen sits down quickly, keeping her eyes to herself.

Carmen had seen a colorful notice tucked between scraps of paper offering bikes for sale, rides to San Francisco, and "cheap" thesis editing on one of the only tangible bulletin boards left just outside her college cafeteria. Curious, she had reached for the paper with one simple word written across the top in calligraphy: *Words*

That had been enough to get her here—that one word, along with a description of a creative writing class, which would urge participants to explore regions of their soul which now lay buried.

Her soul, indeed! What was her soul? Carmen hadn't let her thoughts take her too far into that uncharted territory, as it threatened to be a journey into darkness, pain and utter hopelessness. Her struggle these past years had already been pocked with therapy appointments, missed classes and the most visible blight of all: countless trips to the emergency room, barely surviving copious amounts of narcotics or severe loss of blood.

Why am I even here? she wonders, repressing the urge to run—run far away. What can a creative writing course do for her, much less for her mangled and mutilated soul? She nearly talks herself into making a hasty retreat—long before she would be called to bare any element of her tortured life in front of complete strangers. But her seat partner, a semi-sincere-looking girl by the name of Jade, intrigues her, appearing to be not a day past fourteen. Jade holds just enough magnetism to keep Carmen firmly rooted to her chair. Jade and Mandy, whose caramel voice seems hypnotic as she introduces this class.

"This is your time. You choose what to write and what not to write. There will be no grades. There are no rules about reading your work—unless someone dominates the time and leaves no room for others," she grins.

Mandy's words disarm. Quiet. Reassure. Carmen is not used to a safe invitation, and she wonders, briefly, whether she dares trust this person.

But Mandy leaves her no time to continue engaging her distrustful thoughts.

"First, would any of you like to tell me what brought you here?" Mandy's voice continues.

Momentarily uncomfortable silence.

"A piece of hot pink paper on the bulletin board," a high-pitched voice ventures. Carmen turns slowly to see who else has been attracted by this unconventional invitation.

Mandy smiles. "Welcome."

"I've got lots of words, but most of them mean nothing. I want to find words that connect to something deeper."

"Yeah, and I've *heard* lots of words, and I think I'm *becoming* those words. That scares me. I want to change the words."

With each voice that speaks into this configuration of young, old, male, female, manicured and rumpled, Carmen's anxiety is eased.

Carmen writes seven words the first class. Exactly seven. No more come. The next class, twenty-five; the following, eighteen. Shame drapes itself over her frame as she sits motionless on her chair after every other participant has disappeared.

"Carmen, are you okay?" Mandy asks, sitting down beside her.

The extended silence is punctuated with a sniffle, the toss of her dark hair and the words: "I don't belong."

Mandy waits. Silent. Tasting the pain.

Carmen rises to leave.

"I hope you'll be back."

That was all.

The following week Carmen's absence is noticed by every remaining participant. They have already lost others in prior weeks.

Pens begin scratching on paper. Some heads are down; some faces are upturned in thought. A dark form enters and sits alone in the back. She makes no eye contact.

Noiselessly Mandy walks back and hands her a paper containing six words: *Write anything using the word "scar."*

Carmen pulls a tattered notebook and a pen from her bag. Today she'll possibly write thirty words, she snorts without sound. Thirty words become three hundred; then many hundreds more. She sits; she writes; she sobs; she pounds the desk.

She has written for hours—alone with Mandy, who sits wordlessly three tables over. When words come no more, she lifts her tear-drenched face, realizing for the first time that everyone has gone. Except for Mandy.

Her eyes flash, her voice soars.

"Those scars are not me!
I didn't do that to me.
I didn't beat myself,
     burn myself with cigarette butts.
I didn't rape myself at age three.
I didn't tell myself
     I was ugly, stupid and worthless.
I didn't sell myself to boys next door, uncles,
     pimps, johns...
I didn't fail sixth grade because I had
     recurring bouts with Syphilis

... and many other diseases *they* said I
contracted.
I didn't *contract* them;
      they were *forced* on me.
I didn't break my leg because I
      beat myself mercilessly.
I didn't lie to protect myself from arrest after
      my eyes were black and blue
      ...and swollen shut.
That wasn't me.
That was done *to* me.
I am not one big scar.
I have survived.
I can do this!
No one will force anything on me again!
My word is NEVER.
Never again."

Transcendence

>⌒~

"Momma, I'm gonna be a dancer," she repeated over and over, lips upturned, soft sable eyes glistening as if in a trance.

Every day the same response: nothing. Her mother didn't turn her tousled head that bent over greasy scrambled eggs; she didn't take note as she argued with someone on the phone; she yelled at the young girl's two loudly protesting younger brothers, as their clothes were yanked on before preschool. Ebony could have shouted this announcement from the rooftops—or even the highest spot in their sparse apartment—and still Momma would have just yelled, "Get down from there, d'ya hear!"

But Ebony felt the dancer. She saw her, smelled her, tasted her. Her dreams filled with glistening, shimmering visions of lithe limbs in delicate movement, bathed in ethereal light. Of course, her five-year-old description would simply have been, "pretty."

Her days trudged on, one after another. Gloom, harshness, fear and poverty threatened to asphyxiate her and her five siblings. But Ebony glowed, skipped and whistled—at least after her older brother Sam had taught her how. Whistling then became her favorite pastime, evoking threats to "beat that noise right outta ya" from her beleaguered mother.

"Momma did all she could for my siblings and me," Ebony would later explain with adoring affection. "She had few tools to work with, which meant we all became resilient." That seemed to satisfy all prying and prodding inquirers, and questions would turn to her inspiring gift.

Every opportunity Ebony had, she pushed her body to move, bend, sway, reach and feel: in her bedroom; in the confines of the tiny elementary school bathroom stall; on the sidewalk waiting for a bus. Everywhere.

Ebony could never point to a first time Ms. Cleager addressed her personally, as she rarely paid conscious attention to people when they spoke. She wasn't rude or inattentive, but she had learned to live in her own thoughts, move to her own rhythm, hear her own melody in the midst of deadening distractions.

"Ebony, I think you're a dancer!" were the first words of Ms. Cleager's that reached Ebony's heart.

"Excuse me, ma'am? What did you say?"

The sixth-grade poetry teacher smiled. "Ebony, you're a dancer, aren't you?"

Ebony felt her body shiver and her heart flutter. She caught her breath quickly, "Ms. Cleager, I wish I were. Really, I do. But I've never been to a dance class."

"Ah, my darlin'! A class doesn't make you something you aren't. You can't *learn* to dance any more than you can *learn* to write poetry. It's in your soul! Instruction merely nurtures and guides. Like watering a seedling that's already there."

A holy reverence settled over Ebony. She was a dancer. *She!* Just as she had always known.

"Here," Ms. Cleager handed Ebony a slightly crinkled flyer. "If you're interested, ask your mother if you can come with me."

Ebony didn't wait for an opportune time. She veritably bombarded her mother about dance class as the first, tired foot stepped over the threshold that night. For once, the fact that her mother was mercilessly overwhelmed worked in Ebony's favor.

"She a teacher?" her mother asked after one brief glance. Ebony nodded, holding her breath. "Aw go on, then," and then quickly added, "Just don't come cryin' to me to help with your homework."

"Oh, Momma, thank you! Thank you!" Ebony wrapped her arms around the exhausted woman's ample waist, burying her head in the musty overcoat. Her mother planted two pats on her head—a very rare expression of affection for her only daughter.

"And don't go throwin' all kinda furniture on its head—you flittin' all over this place," she warned.

Ebony's assurances of diligence and caution were profuse as she turned to reflect on her unexpected good fortune alone in her bedroom. She squeezed her eyes tight, whispered a shout, noiselessly sprang up and down, jabbed the air above her head with a closed fist. Her eyes shone in disbelief. She—*she,* Ebony Rose McKnight, would be a *real* dancer.

Ebony lost track of spring, summer, fall and winter. Days turned into weeks and months into years. She maintained her schoolwork, and sometimes went to a basketball game with friends. But her life was consumed with dance. She had classes, performances, drills, remedial work, recitals—every kind of dance configuration possible. She tore ligaments, twisted ankles and fell on already bruised knees. Over time her body became as flexible as a strip of bamboo, her will as strong as steel.

Ebony's remarkable spirit intrigued every dance instructor: She was not learning an art form, her body and soul *was* the dance. Ebony would twirl, bend, sway and glide along with the music, her mind losing all connection with those around her—fellow dancers, instructors and members of an audience alike.

Her venues were mostly stuffy dance studios, packed with other dancers—sometimes nothing more than garishly lit dank basements, lined with folding chairs. But at more fortunate times—places of worship, concert halls and university stages. When she danced, time evaporated, voices went silent, and eyes were transfixed in rapturous delight.

She danced on the beach at sunset the night she bade farewell to her father. Only in recent years had she come to know his quiet spirit and strong soul. No words could express her gratitude for the gift of time spent with him. Too quickly, he was gone. Dutifully she attended his wake, memorial and burial.

But this was her time—alone with the kindred spirit of the one whose genes she carried. She offered her best gift. Overcome with grief and passion, she began to move and sway, closing her eyes to the orange ball that slipped down toward the motionless, glassy horizon. Her heart composed its own melody—blending rapture and terror. Her head lifted, then lowered. Her limbs leaping, bending, running. Arms tracing invisible circles in the mellowing dusk. Turning. Bowing. Worshiping. Through an invisible portal. One with transcendence.

After the Final Curtain

This compilation comes out of years of *bearing witness* to people's stories. There are as many distinct and valuable stories as there are people on this planet. Because we can never tell every story should never hinder us from telling the stories we are capable of telling.

We see hundreds of faces on a regular basis, often having no idea what shapes their lives. There is a story behind each face: some are peaceful; most contain some pain or difficulty. Being aware is the first criteria for being an agent for change.

I chose these twenty-five stories—some idyllic, some painful, some plain, some haunting, some frightening—to offer credibility to everyone's story. My intention is to support girls and women in their (our) quest to overcome, flourish and thrive.

I would be remiss if I did not address the insidious scourge of racism, abuse and violence that lurks and postures in private as well as in the most public and in what should be the most sacred places. Though I write forthrightly and unapologetically about blatant personal as well as systemic abuse, I in no way condone or accept it.

Please allow me to share a personal appeal to each reader: **if you or anyone you are aware of experience(s) or have/has experienced any form of abuse, please speak with a trusted friend and report it through a local or national hotline**.

127

Thank you for joining me in this project. Every effort brings us closer to ensuring safety and healthy opportunities for every girl and woman.

➤ Julia Penner-Zook

About the Author

Julia Penner-Zook has lived in three countries and has taught at church leadership seminars, in high schools, county jails, court mandated parents' groups and domestic violence facilities. She has her Masters degree in Theology and has done most of her continuing educational work in the area of social services, with a focus on recovery after crisis and violence.

She is a strong advocate for children and women, coming from a position of bearing witness, embrace and relentless grace. She is an unshakable believer in "love wins".

Julia already began writing in high school in Canada, encouraged by a brusque, yet enchantingly gracious teacher, Tina Kehler. She has had articles published in both English and German, and presents in both languages.

Julia is a certified life coach, conference speaker and workshop facilitator, has edited numerous books and is an avid reader. When not coaching, reading or writing, she loves to run, drink coffee, visit art museums, enjoy the beach and play with kids. She is married to Rod, has two grown children—a daughter and a son—and five vivacious grandchildren.

Behind Each Face is Julia's first full-length work to be published. To connect with Julia, to inquire about speaking engagements and to read more of her work, visit

http://juliapennerzook.wordpress.com

 j.penner.zook@gmail.com

@J_Pennz

Courtesy: Stacey L Rhoades Photography

21555867R00098

Made in the USA
Middletown, DE
04 July 2015